D0522153

FILE COPY
WITHDRAWN

DO NOT REMOVE

THE THIRD TRUTH

By the same author

THE YEAR OF MIRACLE AND GRIEF
PARTINGS

THE THIRD TRUTH

Leonid Borodin

Translated from the Russian by
Catriona Kelly

COLLINS HARVILL
8 Grafton Street, London w1
1989

COLLINS HARVILL
William Collins Sons & Co. Ltd
London · Glasgow · Sydney · Auckland
Toronto · Johannesburg

BRITISH LIBRARY CATALOGUING IN PUBLICATION DATA

Borodin, Leonid, *1938*–
The third truth
I. Title   II. Tret'ya pravda. *English*
891.73'44 [F]

ISBN 0-00-271813-8

First published by Possev Verlag in 1981
under the title *Tret'ya pravda*
First published in Great Britain
by Collins Harvill, 1989

© Possev Verlag, V. Goracheck K. G., 1981
Copyright in the English translation
© William Collins Sons & Co. Ltd, 1989

Set in Linotron Imprint by
Rowland Phototypesetting Ltd,
Bury St Edmunds, Suffolk
Printed and bound in Great Britain by
William Collins Sons & Co. Ltd, Glasgow.

Translator's Note

This note is intended to make the English-speaking reader aware of certain symbolic meanings in Borodin's Russian text which cannot be represented adequately in English.

The first such symbolic meaning is that given by the title, *Tret'ya pravda*, here perforce translated as *The Third Truth*, a translation which can only convey part of the meaning of the Russian word. Besides simply "truth", *pravda* can mean "truth" in a contingent sense: "accuracy", "rightness", and for this reason Borodin opposes to it the transcendental word *istina* (translated here as "verity" for its Biblical connotations). *Pravda* can also mean "justice", with the adjective *pravdivyi* (just). An additional, and unavoidable, association for the contemporary Russian reader is, of course, that *pravda* is a word enshrined in the ideology of the Soviet Union, since it is the title of the Party daily.

A key Biblical text which uses the words *pravda* and *istina* in the Russian translation is the First Epistle of St John, in which a direct association is made between the Antichrist (a symbol alluded to at the crisis of Borodin's novel) and the denial of truth: "Who is a liar but he that denieth that Jesus is the Christ? He is anti-christ, that denieth the Father and the Son" (1 John 2: 22).

Another important symbolic group consists of the personal names in the novel. The three central characters, Svetlichnaya, Ryabinin and Selivanov, are connected by the similarity of sound of their first names (Yuliana, Ivan and Andrian).

5

Ryabinin's first name links him with St John, and hence with the revelatory traditions of mystical Christianity, as well as with truth as *istina*; whilst Selivanov's surname ties him directly to Ivan, since (though a bona fide Russian surname) it can be fancifully derived from *selit'*, "to give shelter", and *Ivan*: so *Seli-ivanov*, "he who gives shelter to Ivan". Svetlichnaya, for her part, has a surname derived from *svetloe* "radiant", and *litso*, face.

The translator would like to thank many British and Russian friends for advice on questions linguistic, botanical and biological; and to express especial gratitude to John Richmond for help that was much more than advisory.

C.K.

ONE

Down the road, along the fences of the village of Ryabinovka, went Selivanov, pretending to be tired and lame. Whenever he had to cross a puddle he would stop, raise his foot, grumbling and wheezing, then step right in it anyway and moan and groan, though there was no one to see or hear him.

Selivanov loved to play-act. He'd been doing it all his life. The home-made birch walking stick which he carried had blackened and split, he'd been play-acting so long. Even he wouldn't have been able to say when this had become a habit; the fact is, he didn't think of himself as pretending at all. Had he owned up to this sin and tried racking his memory, it would have meant digging back into his earliest years when he was out hunting with his father: if he missed a shot, he would pull off his shirt and search for a non-existent ant, which, so he said, had "gone and nipped him right in the hairs of the armpit" just as he was about to fire. When his father gave him a clip round the ear all the same, or even the occasional sound smack on the rump, he'd somehow contrive to find a real live ant, which he'd stick right under his father's nose before tearing its head off in revenge.

In just the same way, from his earliest childhood he'd known how to act the fool, play dumb about something, pretend to be sick or shortsighted; he'd been able to walk past a neighbour, for instance, without recognising him, and then when he was greeted, apologise with apparent sincerity and put on a show of mortification. After a drinking bout with friends, he was capable of putting on God knows whose tatty overcoat and leaving his own perfectly presentable one behind; then, after rectifying the mistake, he'd get all distressed: "Well, there you go. They say that's what the bottle leads to, losing one thing after another. Well, that's just me all over!"

Among people who were none too sharp-eyed, he passed for an eccentric; others, who guessed he was putting it on, said that Selivanov shouldn't be trusted further than you could throw him, and kept well clear of him. But nobody could fathom him, not even his father, with whom he'd roamed the *taiga* a little short of ten years – even he couldn't make out his own son, but just gave him a morose look whenever the boy "tried it on".

For all that, there was no malice in Selivanov. If he managed to pull the wool over someone's eyes, he certainly took no pleasure or pride in his own cunning. No, it was simply a compulsion he wasn't conscious of. If his play-acting often worked to his advantage, he also indulged in it when he had nothing to gain by it at all.

Just now, for instance, as he passed the end of the lane, he saw a little girl breaking off rowan branches. He sneaked up behind her and lightly touched her shoulder with his stick. The little girl shrieked and leapt away. Selivanov shook his head, and in a quavering, elderly voice told her off for not treating the tree with respect, since it was decorative and gave pleasure to the village. Now Selivanov actually cared for the village and the tree about as much as he did for the expanses of the Khamar-Daban ridge on the far horizon; but at the moment he was playing the grumpy old sour-puss, who loves to sit by a warm stove and enjoy a natter by the back door, but who loves nothing better than telling young people what to do.

The village of Ryabinovka was so called, they said, for the *ryabina*, rowan tree, thickets thereabouts – in every lane and by every homestead. But that wasn't the whole story . . .

In one part of the village, where the rowans suddenly gave

way, almost without warning, to ancient, crooked Siberian pines, stood Ivan Ryabinin's five-sided house. There was not an old man or woman living in the village who could recall – or whose grandparents had told of – a time when this house had not stood in the village and had not belonged to Ryabinins.

It was towards this house that Andrian Nikanorych Selivanov was now making his way. The path was not short – it crossed from one end of the village to the other – but Selivanov did not hurry. On the contrary, the closer he came to the Ryabinovka house, the more often he stopped for every little thing, the fussier became his gait. But his pace never increased.

For twenty-five years, the Ryabinin house had been empty, and though it hadn't been taken apart plank by plank over this time which as far as house maintenance goes might as well be a thousand years (there were reasons for this, of course), none the less its aspect and bearing had suffered from the sheer lack of a proprietor, especially round the outside: the kitchen garden had reverted to bird cherry and rowan, the yard become the domain of nettles, burdock and agrimony growing impudently in the wide open space, whilst the well had simply grown stagnant and its shoring had collapsed inside.

One of the first administrative acts of each new chairman of the village *soviet* was to proclaim his decision to transfer the three-tenths of a hectare plot to whoever in the village might need it; but every time this happened, a few days would pass, and the same needy person would publicly give up his claim to the "Ryabinin waste ground" – as they called it – and the chairman himself would dismiss the plot from his mind. The inhabitants of Ryabinovka would exchange meaningful looks when anyone in the street or a village shop started to talk about the plot's strange history. The whole business stank of secrecy, and a secret can give significance to all who are party to it. And the secret wasn't the half of it!

Fate had treated Ivan Ryabinin unkindly, unjustly. And though this didn't stir a single soul enough to speak out, nor raise one hand in his defence – sighs, a shake of the head and an involuntary shrug of the shoulders were all he got – none the less everyone had the bitter fate of Ivan Ryabinin etched on mind and memory. To all those who knew and remembered Ivan Ryabinin, the many years' neglect of the "Ryabinin waste ground" had become not merely a justification for their indifference to someone else's misery (they had even become hardened to their own), but a vindication for all that fate is (when fate is unkind), and for everything nameless and beyond reach that lies behind this fate. With time, the inhabitants of Ryabinovka had exaggerated the importance of those three-tenths of a hectare of nettle, burdock and rowan to the fate of their village as a whole; with hints, winks, tut-tuts and clucks and ostentatious coughs they tried to weave their own legend, a legend without words or substance, but full of meaning and unknowable wisdom.

They would have been offended, even angry, if they'd known that there was nothing more to the whole secret than this: every time there was a new claimant to the plot, the man with the birch stick (who was now wandering through the village towards the very house) would appear, clutching a sable to his bosom (if the claimant was greedy), or a bottle of *samogon** (if he was a man's man), or letting fly with a few "well-chosen words" at night by the wicker fence (if he was a coward). And all the former chairmen of the village *soviet* made such a big thing of not greeting Selivanov when they met him that they probably had a tale or two to tell as well.

How many games had the village children played in the thickets during the twenty-five years that the Ryabinin house had stood with its windows boarded up? How many courting couples had sat by the Ryabinin well, how many cats had wooed and wedded in the cobweb jungle of Ryabinin's high loft, how many fledglings had been raised and had taken to the wing from the cracks and holes in the steep-pitched roof . . . !

---

* *samogon:* illegally home-distilled high-proof vodka (usually potato-based).

A generation of Ryabinovka people had been born and brought up while the Ryabinin house stood neglected. Even those who had been born before that had grown used to the boarded-up windows and the obscurity of the owner. So from the morning the old woman Svetlichnaya had let out a gasp outside the shop, slapped her thighs, sat down on the pavement by the side of the road, her eyes bulging at the old man with a knapsack on his back, and whispered fearfully, crossing herself as though she'd seen a ghost: "Oh Lord, that can't be Ivan Ryabinin come back!"; from that very moment, a week ago now, the whole village had been anxiously tut-tutting, throwing up its hands and sniffing loudly.

But when the village had found its tongue again, everyone had started talking volubly: and of course there were the know-alls who would shake their heads with great meaning, and with great significance utter the same phrase, "Twenty-five! T-t-t-twenty-five, eeeh!" And those who were smarter still, who'd been through fire and water blindfolded and with their hands tied behind their back, explained that twenty-five, well, that was the same as a twenty-five rouble note. And that's a bit more than a tenner, isn't it now! And each of them tried to imagine the last twenty-five years as if they hadn't lived them like that at all; but they were unable to imagine their lives in this monstrous new form, and couldn't understand Ivan Ryabinin, who had gone through all this. So they didn't go up to him and congratulate him on his return, for they did not know whether it was appropriate to congratulate someone in such circumstances.

No one approached Ivan Ryabinin that day, nor the next, nor the third. On the fourth day he himself emerged and was spotted at once by half the village; people stood stock still, holding their breath, as if Ryabinin had come out to shame them all over something or to settle the score with somebody. But then he went to the village *soviet* and stayed there for no more than half an hour, and came out just as quietly, not looking at anyone, not greeting anyone.

That was when the village remembered everything it had forgotten about him, or not bothered to remember, before. And these forgotten facts suddenly became more than an interesting and romantic story; they became part of history, the way some events stand out from the rest as the genuine, spontaneous history of the people, irrespective of whether or not the people participated in them.

The village felt remorse, but was tormented more by the fact that it was not *conscious* of wrong-doing and suspected that it had done no wrong; nevertheless, it felt guilty, as people do in the presence of a cripple. It followed him past the house to the outskirts accompanied by the sly gaze of dozens of small boys; it spoke, it lapsed into silent thought. At some time during that earlier period separated from the present by twenty-five years, people had dealings with Ryabinin – as a ranger, he had dealt with many people; these people were now enjoying general esteem. All of them tried to conjure up good feelings towards the ranger, but all in vain – on the contrary, it turned out that each one of them had suffered at least one brush with the stern guardian of the Ryabinovka *taiga*.

The old women wrinkled their brows as the village cast its mind back and recalled Ivan Ryabinin's mother – a fussy, nimble woman – and his father, too, who had not returned from the Civil War; he'd been off somewhere by the sea, where he'd fought for the Reds against two of his own elder sons who'd been among the Kappelites* and who'd fallen without trace during those years so gluttonous of human life. The village remembered Ivan as a small boy, hard-working, invariably sullen, a solitary orphan, who had turned into a tough, strapping lad without anybody noticing; he'd become first a forester, and then the first *soviet* ranger. With the benefit of hindsight, the village was now ready to admit that Ivan Ryabinin had always been fair in his duties as a ranger, and only

* "Kappelites": nickname of remnants of the force of General Vladimir Oskarovich Kappel (1883–1920), the leader of the White Third Army in its retreat to Omsk, 1919; killed in retreat from Irkutsk the following year.

put the squeeze on people who pillaged the *taiga* outrageously. But to acknowledge this wasn't easy, because how could you forget the vicious looks a culprit could give Ivan Ryabinin when the *militsia** took him away? How could you forget the village's avid frenzy as it fell upon the bounty of the *taiga* during the short interregnum, and the sly pleasure with which people screwed up their eyes when they understood that if you gave the new ranger a bottle of *samogon* he was ready to turn a blind eye on a whole forest tract, let alone on half a dozen spindly pines, and let you blast away at as much gamefowl as you wanted? For several years a bottle of *samogon* had been the only currency in the *taiga*, and the village had grown fat and flabby on its lawlessness. But then even the village was ready to think again; the village hunters shook their heads, clicked their tongues and grunted, as they cast nasty sidelong looks at the ranger's new house. And long might they have cast such looks if, absurd to relate, the blundering ranger hadn't been trampled by a broad-antlered elk in its death-throes.

Then for the first time the village cast its mind back to Ivan Ryabinin with approval. The recollection, though, was brief: human life is not so much still water as a river in full spate, and it takes skill to live and survive. Not a simple matter, when it seems as if the whole world beyond the edge of the village has bared its teeth in inexplicable ferocity, has set out snares devised by Satan himself for the perdition of man.

The village recalled that fine summer's day when the Swan Princess had appeared on the porch of the Ryabinin house. She'd emerged from the doorway as if born the minute before, in the moment the door scraped open, with her golden hair and her dainty white feet. Everything confirmed the miracle of her birth: the way she screwed up her eyes against the sunshine, then shut them as if pondering some private secret; the way Ivan Ryabinin looked at her, all perplexity and amazement, pausing by the wood-pile with his axe at rest; the way

* *militsia:* the Soviet police force.

13

they then came together on the bottom step of the porch, silent, not touching each other. No one could remember now who it was in the village who had seen the birth of this miracle in the Ryabinin house. For a lone wolf like Ryabinin to steal a city princess was something the village hadn't expected, and, at first, there were those who'd taken offence and pursed their lips, ready to show stout opposition to the ranger's challenge. However, the challenge was never uttered, and the village could only detect it dimly in his aloofness. Ryabinin was in no hurry to show himself to the people with his young lady, and she regarded the fence round his plot not as a fence, but as a barrier, as though the last thing she meant to do was to pass through that wicket gate and out of the fortress of wattle fencing, within which she saw her happiness and fortune.

The path which went past the Ryabinin house into the *taiga* was not the only path, nor even the most convenient; but that summer everyone, the women going out for bilberries, men going about their forest craft, or children out after garlic, everyone seemed to choose that path, even if it meant a detour of more than a mile, just to get a glimpse of the "foreigner" and the chance to wag their tongues and chatter about what that ranger of theirs was up to.

Remembering this after a score of years and more, the village felt it could rightly be proud of the way it had treated this stranger; of how, after the ranger had brought a sewing-machine from town, the wives and village girls, without prejudice or envy, had taken trunkfuls of cloth remnants saved from NEP times* in the twenties along to the ex-city seamstress; and how when they'd received dresses, skirts and jackets of a not entirely usual cut in return, they hadn't grumbled but had been unstinting with payments in cash and in kind.

A little more than a year passed, and the men and women who took the path heard a child's cry in the Ryabinin house;

* NEP: New Economic Policy (1921–5): period when limited scope was allowed to private enterprise in the production and sale of consumer goods.

and the village was not offended when the name that Ivan gave his little daughter, Natalya, was one which no one in the village had had in living memory.

But when the ranger's wife's figure was swelling for a second time, mounted *militsia* appeared and took Ivan Ryabinin off to town, where he vanished without trace. For a whole day and night, it seemed, the village didn't take its eyes off the windows of the Ryabinin house. When morning came, and revealed that the house was boarded up on all sides, and that even the wicket gate was barred, everyone was amazed. There was a flood of rumours, most of which the village has forgotten today; none the less one persistent rumour stuck in its memory – that at the crack of dawn the day after they'd taken the ranger away, someone had seen a heavily loaded horse-drawn cart on the back road, and in it the ranger's wife in tears and with a baby in her arms, while some village man, urging on a bay mare, comforted her with rough words.

Selivanov had already rounded the last house, that is the second-to-last house, because the very last, beyond the bushy rowan, was the house he was heading for while trying so hard not to hurry.

Something – Selivanov couldn't recall a feeling like it ever before – possessed him with each successive step towards the Ryabinin house. Never in his entire life had fear or good fortune (and he'd known fear more than once in his life) left his hands shaking like this or gripped his chest so much that he wanted to sit down on the ground. On one side, off the path, he saw the fallen trunk of a birch tree. He stepped up to it, prodding it with his stick, digging into the rotten wood beneath just in case an adder might be lurking there (they love rotten birch-wood, adders do), and sat down, not shamming this time, but seized with a real attack of panting, though he'd been walking much too slowly to have brought it on.

It would be as well to sit a while and recall what must be recalled before crossing the threshold of that house, which a miracle had now brought back to life. But Selivanov needed no effort to recall it; he had forgotten nothing. One vision after another stung his memory; each was separate, unlinked – or rather, there was a kind of link, but one that existed all on its own; the link was life itself, as Selivanov had known it and had nothing to do with memory. And it would be a lie indeed to call the narrative which now follows Andrian Nikanorych's "reminiscences", because reminiscences, even in the most detailed and conscientious paraphrase, are both more and less than what happened in reality. Not all feelings can be subjected to words, not all that happens is accessible to feeling; something always remains beyond its boundaries, part of the feelings of someone else who was also present or who could have been present, as it were.

TWO

It was winter; the *taiga* was covered in snowdrifts and two men were moving fast across it. One was beginning to gain on the other. The man in front was a short, puny, bustling creature, the man behind was tall, broad-shouldered and burly, and together they resembled nothing so much as a human hunter in pursuit of his animal quarry.

Seen sideways on, the chase hardly resembled a chase at all, because the gait of the man in front, his every movement, even the rhythmic thwacking of his home-made elk-fur-covered skis on the snow, insidiously conveyed his impudent confidence that he would get away. But the man chasing him was just as certain that he would catch up, for was he not a *taiga* dweller; moreover he was still at an age where he had yet to discover the limits of his own strength – he still thought his powers inexhaustible. "All right, run then!" muttered the man in the rear. "You won't get far, you're as frail as a rotten twig!" "Come on, come on," the man in front sniggered, looking round cockily. "Watch yourself now, remember the one about the bull who was chasing a hare but ended up with a hare-lip himself!"

The truth of the matter was that the one really did have to get away at all costs, whilst the other had resolved to catch him if he had to run a hundred leagues to do it, because it would be a long time before he got a chance like this again.

For two seasons in a row Andrian Selivanov had been raiding forest ranger Ivan Ryabinin's patrol sector, and this time he'd run slap bang into the ranger himself. For two seasons the ranger had been tracking this cunning poacher and law-breaker. Now at last he'd caught him red-handed: he had the stuff in a knapsack which was bobbing tantalisingly in front of the ranger's eyes, now fifty yards beyond his reach, now a hundred. At one point he'd nearly had it in his grasp, but then Selivanov had broken off a branch and flung it down in front of his pursuer's skis.

Selivanov was ski-ing on the fresh powder-snow, and the ranger was following in his tracks, but he had little joy of it. Snow crumbling down from the borders of the track stopped his skis from biting. Moreover, Selivanov had picked a route through a thicket of birch saplings with branches so close to the ground that even he had to crouch low, scuttling like a mouse.

Ryabinin forced his way through with the butt and barrel of his rifle, but he was not always quick enough to turn his face away from the slashing cuts of the birch branches. He felt no pain, but it still held him back, so that he lost the advantage he'd gained when he was ski-ing in the open on sloping ground and on hard-packed snow.

Selivanov was hoping to get clear of the ranger in the birch thicket on the furthest slope and then make for the village, since there was an unwritten law that the ranger's power and his rights as a *taiga*-dweller ended at the village boundary.

For his part, Ryabinin had guessed the intentions of this poacher who'd given him such trouble for two seasons, and was sure that he'd catch up with him in the field on the edge of the village. Indeed, he had to. He knew, of course, that his law was more powerful than the law of the village, and that he could simply arrest Selivanov, booty and all, in his own house, and no one would dare to stand in his way; he knew that it didn't matter a scrap if the entire village, from babes in arms to wrinkled grandads, were going to hate his guts for it. He knew all this, but he also knew that this wasn't the point. It was before he reached the village that he had to catch Selivanov and drag him there by the scruff of the neck. Once there he could even let him go, after rubbing his nose in the snow a few times – that didn't matter. But he did have to catch him, otherwise nobody would respect him.

There was another reason why the ranger's blood was up. Selivanov hadn't got up to his dirty tricks just anywhere in his patrol sector: he'd had the nerve to trespass in his, the ranger's own private patch. Ryabinin had found Selivanov's traces right there in his salting shed; Selivanov had had the barefaced cheek to cut up a Manchurian deer, a protected species, in the ranger's own cabin. He hadn't even bothered to cover his tracks or to clear up – it was just as if he'd stuck two fingers up at the ranger. For ages now Ryabinin's mighty fists had been itching to lay into Selivanov.

With barely a hundred paces separating them they reached the top of the last gentle slope; a hundred yards or so further, the downhill run with its covering of birches would begin. Here Selivanov put on a spurt. Brushing the branches away with the butt of his father's Sauer shotgun, he stooped to the waist and headed for the thickest clumps of birches. Staring straight ahead all the time, concentrating every muscle on flight, Selivanov felt as though his head were poking way out in front of his skis. The slope began abruptly, and he went off looping and zig-zagging downhill, cutting his turns as tight as he could and tossing a branch or two down behind him so that the ranger would be jolted out of his tracks as he skied down. When the ground levelled off for a little and interrupted his descent, Selivanov looked round and grunted with satisfaction: the ranger had fallen behind.

But down in the hollow, where the snowdrifts were three-foot deep and the pine trees had boles two-span round and tips that seemed to touch the sky, fate played him a nasty trick. Well, what else but fate? – he'd made no mistakes himself. He'd avoided the drifts unerringly, giving the damn things a good six-foot berth. But who could have known that the feeble winter wind had snapped a miserable branch off one of the pines and that it was lying, camouflaged by a sprinkling of snow and held fast in the surface, like a snare across his path? One of his feet got caught in it, the other slid inertly over the top, and Selivanov fell straight on his nose in the drift as if he'd been lassooed.

It took time to pick himself up, more time to shake the snow off. And imagine trying to drag a ski out against the grain of the fur! The ranger was almost upon him. You couldn't see him in the birch thicket, but you could hear the crackle of branches and the crunch of snow.

Selivanov could still have got away: he could either have shrugged off his knapsack and thrown the filthy deer-hide in the snow, or he could have trodden the skin into the snow and made a dash for it, a hundred yards or so, and waited for the ranger to catch up with him. But Selivanov had been terrified of fights since he was a lad. He wasn't afraid of anything in the *taiga*: bears, lynxes, didn't bother him, nor did darkness and foul weather. But his father's beatings, the fights he'd had with other lads in his village, and even drunken punch-ups caused him pain in mind and body. He couldn't even watch other people fighting without fear and trembling. Perhaps that was why he kept out of people's way, why the *taiga* had become his beloved home, a place where he could keep out of harm's way winter and summer.

And now, as he imagined himself face to face with this great bear of a ranger, a man who'd dragged cows out of the bog by the horns almost before he was able to walk, Selivanov struggled and twitched to haul himself frantically out of the drift. Having finally freed his leg, he tore off towards the broadest pine-trunk he could see.

"Don't come any closer!" he shrieked, as Ryabinin executed his last turn and skied down into the hollow. "Don't come any closer, or I'll blow you away!"

"Just you wait!" the ranger answered, letting his breath out in a slow hiss. He spoke out loud but his voice was calm with hidden menace, and Selivanov went weak at the knees, hearing him speak like this.

"I'll blow you sky-high!" he shouted insistently, and squeezed the trigger of his Sauer, without having time to take aim or even raise the butt to his shoulder. The kick of the gun threw him back behind the pine, and he almost lost his balance. When he looked round the tree again, he saw the ranger thrashing about in the snow.

"So I *have* blown him sky-high!" he said to himself in a startled whisper, and was about to step forward when he saw the dark muzzle of the ranger's rifle looking at him like the pupil of an eye. He stepped back behind the pine again and was seized by a fit of the shakes. It wasn't the shot itself; it was the way the giant pine tree vibrated when the bullet struck it full in its frozen trunk. He looked out again round the other side, and this time the bullet tore off a piece of the trunk, spraying his face with splinters. He started to reason feverishly. He'd fired at the ranger from the left barrel, so he must have sprayed him with buckshot . . . He hadn't aimed, so he could only have hit him with a couple of pieces of shot, if that. Or then again, perhaps he hadn't hit him at all, perhaps he'd just lain down anyway, although it wasn't like him to do that.

"Hey!" Selivanov shouted, this time staying behind the trunk. The only reply was another shot, but one that didn't shake the pine tree.

"Stop firing, will you!" yelled Selivanov, more loudly this time. He bent down until his face was touching the snow, took off his fur hat and peeked out with one eye. Ryabinin tried to get up, holding his rifle at the ready with one hand, but cried out and fell back on to the snow again, sinking so deeply into the drift that the barrel of his rifle pointed at the sky.

"So I have hit him!" he whispered. He still hadn't quite taken in what had happened; his brain was just beginning to get to grips with it.

The ranger looked like a bear emerging from its den as he

struggled in the snow, and Selivanov took fright again. He took the gun in his hands, but the next minute flung it down behind the pine. The muzzle fell flat, and Ryabinin's head appeared above the snowdrift. Selivanov could even see his face, twisted either with rage or with pain.

"Hey, listen, we must have a talk!" shouted Selivanov, pleading now.

"I'll give you talk, you swine!" bawled Ryabinin, and fired.

"Now what are you wasting cartridges for? Where've I hit you, then?"

Ryabinin said nothing, but felt with his left hand for his hip, where Selivanov's pellet had lodged, or maybe passed straight through. It was as if a knitting needle had gone into his leg and was sticking out of it, stopping him from getting up on to his skis, which had sunk right down to the bottom of the snowdrift.

"Listen, we must talk!" shouted Selivanov again. "Where've I hit you, then? Say something, will you! I'm no killer! I fired because I was scared, that's all!"

"Just you come out from behind there, and I'll blow you away myself!" the ranger's voice echoed.

"Can't you get up, then?" asked Selivanov. He meant his voice to sound sympathetic, but as he had to yell to be heard, the question sounded more like a taunt.

"You won't get away from here either!" Ryabinin answered furiously. He'd finally managed to reach his wound with his hand and he could feel blood.

"Won't get away, indeed!" Selivanov shouted. "Course I will. All I have to do is keep behind this pine tree here!"

The ranger realised that Selivanov really could get away if he used the pine tree as cover. In his desperation he fired two more shots in succession, then twisted round to get another cartridge clip out of his pouch. But Selivanov had been keeping count of his shots, and as soon as he heard the last chips hit the snow, he sprang from behind the pine and rushed towards Ryabinin. The ranger had the cartridge clip in his hand and had already got the cartridge chamber open, but Selivanov was too quick for him. Ryabinin shook all over and grimaced as the rifle was grabbed from his hand.

"Swine!" he whispered, looking at Selivanov sitting two paces away.

"If you want to die, it's up to you," said Selivanov calmly. At last he felt he had the situation under control. "But if you don't, let's make a deal! No use getting worked up for nothing. I never meant to kill you! But if you'd've caught me, you'd've knocked all my teeth out on to the snow! That's true, isn't it, now?"

"What do you want?" Ryabinin asked angrily.

"Did I get you in the leg?"

"What do you want?" the ranger repeated.

"What do I want? I'll strap up your leg and get you back to my house, then I'll make you better – it'll heal up a treat, just like my dogs' cuts always do. But don't you try anything on."

"Try anything on! After you've peppered me with shot!"

"Live and let live," said Selivanov, shrugging. Then he added uncertainly, "Now if you want anything else from me . . . some money, maybe . . . or anything else you fancy . . ."

He lowered his brows and looked down at Ryabinin.

"I'll do anything you like, just tell me what . . ."

"Well, you can get on with cutting through my breeks, then!"

Selivanov flung himself down, tore off his skis, and went up to the ranger, floundering thigh-deep in the snow. He took the knapsack off Ryabinin's back, stamped down the snow all round, turned him over on his back and gently prodded his legs.

"Here?"

Ryabinin screwed up his face.

"Gone through your thigh, has it? Can you not get up at all, then? Well, we *must* get you up, though!" Selivanov deliberated, cutting through Ryabinin's trouser leg rapidly and delicately with his knife, and looking askance at the patch of scarlet on the snow.

The shot had gone through Ryabinin's thigh at an angle and come out at the side, leaving a jagged wound. Ryabinin made an effort to prop himself up and have a look, but Selivanov stopped him with a gentle shove, sending him on to his back again. "Ouch, you swine!" the ranger whispered, hardly able to contain his rage. He turned away from Selivanov.

"That's right, you call me all the names you like!" muttered Selivanov, tearing a piece of rag lengthwise and laying it on the exit wound from below. "Well, there's no good in trying to blow a man from your own village away, but I'm telling you, I did it 'cos I was scared! Look here, see how big your fist is next to mine! If you'd tried doing me over, you'd have finished my liver for sure. I'd have been spewing blood. Now, just let me put this ointment on you – I've made it from pine resin – and the wound'll heal up so you'll never see the scar after . . . You'll be springing around like a young goat in a week. Hold on now, whilst I strap you up!"

The ranger heeded neither his words nor his actions. "Give me my mittens!" he said under his breath. "My hands are frozen."

Selivanov picked up the mittens, which were lying one on top of the other on the snow, and was about to pass them over, but then he felt how damp they were. He passed over his own instead, and Ryabinin tried to pull them on. "How can I get these on my hands? I'd have trouble even fitting them on my you-know-what!" He chucked them away and blew on his fingers.

Selivanov got a sable skin out of his knapsack, smoothed it out and sliced through it in several places with studied carelessness, as if to say he couldn't give a damn about it. He wound it round each of the ranger's hands, then took off Ryabinin's fur hat, brushed the snow off, and put it on him again, pulling it down over his ears, saying as he did so:

"You may have the strength of a wild boar, but you're a

weakling all the same! That little hole in you's nothing to worry about, it would never have put *me* off the track! Just look at you sprawling there like a felled tree . . ."

He didn't have a chance to finish speaking. The ranger grabbed him by the skirt of his coat, held him at arm's length with one hand and, taking hold of the scruff of his neck with the other, shoved him into the snow a couple of times right up to the nape of his neck and then pushed him away. Shaking snow off himself and spitting it out, wheezing and letting out sham coughs and sneezes, Selivanov crawled to a safe distance and only then risked moaning in a hurt and plaintive tone, "What about our deal? If you've shoved my face in the snow now, I bet you'll be shoving it in the fence as soon as I've dragged you home, right?"

Ryabinin tried to get up, but something in his leg really didn't seem to be working properly. It wouldn't do what he told it. Cursing angrily, he collapsed on his back again.

"Well then. Do you want to fight or don't you?" asked Selivanov crossly.

"That's enough of your lip! Get a fire going, will you, 'fore I freeze to death!"

"That's better, now," Selivanov nodded, satisfied.

Selivanov flattened out another patch about a yard away from Ryabinin, and began to collect twigs and sticks to throw on it. Soon he'd got a little bonfire going. The ranger stretched himself out towards it. "You've done for one of my tendons, you swine! I hope to God I won't get a limp!"

"Pooh, course you won't," Selivanov waved the idea away. "I'll soon cobble something together so I can drag you back home. Then I'll give you some of my tonic I make from roots. Just you wait, you'll never have had anything like that before, I bet. And to think you were hunting me down, eh! It's enough to make me laugh. I should be the ranger, you know, I'd teach those men in the village how to behave! I've been here since I could toddle, you know. You've never had sight nor sniff of half the things I know about the *taiga*."

"Bullshit!" answered Ryabinin, all anger now gone from his voice.

"What do you mean, bullshit?" Selivanov was offended. "Didn't I manage to get sables out from under your nose two winters in succession?"

"What do you do with their skins? Why don't you hand them over, like you're supposed to?" asked the ranger, frowning.

"Who says *supposed to*, Vanya?" said Selivanov, all innocence.

"The powers that be, that's who!"

"Well, I don't know about your dad, but I know my dad, and his dad and grandad before him, all lived off the *taiga*, and there were no 'powers that be' that had any say in the *taiga*! They lived their lives, and that was all there was to it. And now the powers that be, that is you, have turned up and you say, 'It's mine!' But why should it be yours, when before it always belonged to us? And there's no power set over those powers that be to decide what *we've* a right to!"

"Are you saying you don't acknowledge those powers?" Ryabinin looked askance.

"I keep myself to myself, so should they!" said Selivanov, screwing up his eyes.

"So you want to get rich, do you?"

Selivanov answered this question with another question.

"Why don't you get married? I've heard them say none of the girls in Ryabinovka can find any way to tie you down."

"None of your business!"

"Egsakly! So you see, it's not right for everyone to know everyone else's business."

"Lost your nerve, did you, when you fired at me? Not so easy killing a man as a Manchurian deer, eh?"

Selivanov screwed up his eyes, putting on a sly and shifty face.

"I can shoot some little git as easy as I can crap on my own finger, Vanya. But to shoot a real man, that's a terrible thing and no mistake! But you know I didn't really aim at you, I just fired the gun. Well, see, I was scared. The shot went all over the place, so you got hit. I was afraid of your big fists. I knew what you had in mind for me, see! That buck I gralloched in your cabin, just that one buck would've been enough to make you hoik my eye out and hang it on a twig."

"You're right there!" the ranger assured him. "Why did you have to make such a mess? Or didn't you know what was coming to you if you did things like that?"

"I don't know myself what made me do such wicked things," replied Selivanov, none too truthfully. "Well, I'm off to make something for you to ride on now. It's already getting late, and it'll be no fun shifting you! I must hurry."

He cut down plenty of six-foot branches and laid them out evenly in the snow. He wound thin whippy birch boughs and lengths of string round the ends and the middle, fixed Ryabinin's ski bindings on at the sides, and attached a pulling strap at the end, using his own gun-sling to make it. He doused the bonfire with snow and then went up to the ranger.

"Time we were off, Vanya! Put on your mittens, they've dried out. Now, hang on!"

He squatted down in front of Ryabinin. Ryabinin put his arms round his shoulders and hauled himself up on to his good leg. Selivanov let out a grunt. "Phew, you're heavy, you can't weigh less than sixteen stone! *I've* never been an ounce over ten, not even when I've been stuffing myself."

It was no more than two normal paces to Selivanov's improvised sledge, but they only just made it. Ryabinin slumped down on to the sledge clumsily, landing on his side. Selivanov opened his eyes wide and let out a sigh of relief.

He put the two guns next to the ranger, secured them, and fixed both knapsacks under Ivan's head. Snorting noisily, he flung the strap over his chest. Tensing his muscles with the effort, he moved the sledge off with a jerk, then stopped and turned to the ranger with an expression of satisfaction. "I can do it! Good job it's winter, not summer, and downhill, I'll say . . ."

He shook his head and, bending nearly to the ground, set off. He hauled the sledge along the hollow so as to skirt the birch thicket. He'd intended to go through it to get away from the ranger, but with the burden he had now, it was impassable. But Selivanov knew every last tree-stump in the area, and soon a cutting or summer footpath could be seen opening out of the dip. At the moment it was covered in snow and there were no tracks. Along here Selivanov made his way. When the descent became steep, he flung the strap off his shoulders and pulled at the sledge very gently. It was hard to stop it sliding away from him. Now and then the sledge jolted sideways, got stuck in the snow. A few times Ryabinin fell off, but Selivanov unceremoniously bundled him back on to the branches and continued to haul, ignoring Ryabinin's cursing.

When the descent ended and they were out in the open, the village came into view in the distance. Selivanov, by now plastered with sweat, came to a halt, took off his hat, unbuttoned his coat and sat down on the snow, groaning and spreading his legs. The ranger, too, looked round in relief, wrinkling his face with pain, and brushing the snow off his face as it melted like runnels of icy sweat.

"There now!" Selivanov said boastfully. "Now the time I dragged my dad back from Chekhardak in 'twenty with his chest shot through, now that really was work, let me tell you! I dragged him back alive over two rises and dead over two more. Never looked him in the face, just kept dragging away like I'd gone bananas. Then I heard him stop groaning, you know, but I still went on hauling. I was young then, see, had no sense . . . Really made me mad I was dragging a dead man!"

"Who did him in then?" asked Ryabinin, not specially interested.

"Who in?"

"Your father, who else?"

Selivanov sniffed and squinted at the ranger.

"Well, it was one of those things, you know . . ."

"All right then, don't tell me! Get on with pulling me now, I'm fair freezing to death!"

The village of Luchikha where Selivanov lived (or where it was officially considered that he did) was about six miles along the river Ledyanka from Ryabinovka, going downstream. But Ryabinovka was a bit out of the way, and it wasn't on the road leading to Piney Dale and then on to Lake Baikal and Irkutsk. It was to Luchikha that Selivanov was taking the ranger now, although Ryabinovka was closer. Well, you could see why: he was hardly going to look for help in the ranger's own village. The men there might be pretty fed up with the ranger's doings, but they weren't going to take an outsider's part either. So now Selivanov was dragging the ranger back to "his" house, which he'd bought a few years back. In fact the house had an unlived in, neglected look, and the wood hadn't been renewed as it should have been. It was only Selivanov's in the sense that it was his registered address; winter and summer he actually spent in his secret cabins at the *taiga*.

In the co-operative where Selivanov was registered they'd long ago thrown up their hands and given him up as a bad job. Or at any rate, the president had, since Selivanov's generosity kept his palm well greased. The president was half-blind, lame and feared the *taiga* as much as the Devil fears holy water. But for all that he was a shrewd accountant with a specially sharp eye for fur; he knew a great deal about fur and revelled in simply looking at it. Selivanov was contemptuous of this passion, but did as much as he could, and as much as was necessary, to fan the flames. For Selivanov himself had only one joy in life: to be able to live according to his own desire and whim, and to make his own tracks in the *taiga*, or at the very least have no one snooping on his tail.

Selivanov loved power, but he wasn't interested in having power over other people. Their souls were more twisted than the twistiest woodland paths, they were unstable and unreliable and you couldn't feel secure and at peace among them. You had to be on your guard all the time, or you'd suddenly end up with a lot of unnecessary fuss and bother.

Now the *taiga*, that was another thing altogether! When summer ended, winter always followed, and in winter snow always fell. It was never any different. You could follow the paths without thinking. They'd never let you down, there were no dead-ends, and when you got to a stream you'd always found the path continuing on the other bank, exactly opposite. And as for your tongue, better to keep it well behind your teeth in company, because words could be understood in so many different ways. Suddenly you'd see people looking askance, pursing their lips, and that meant trouble! Strain every nerve to avoid it; be cunning or sly, pretend for all you were worth, give in or hold out, run away or stay put; what was the use in the end?

But in the *taiga* a man always had a one-to-one relationship, just him and the *taiga*. Once he understood the language the *taiga* spoke, then there was no end to the loving talk he could have. Selivanov was drunk with power in the *taiga*, because there was nothing there which he wasn't master of. Moreover, he didn't have to struggle to reassert his power whenever he returned; he just went back and took over again. If it was a wild beast you were dealing with, you had the barrels of your gun; if it was a tree, you had an axe; if you heard rustling, you had your ears, if you wanted to see into the distance, you had your eyes. You had joy to appreciate the beauty, and skill to overcome the dangers.

When the road away from other people turned into a forest path, and the path narrowed so it was only wide enough for one man – the man who had made it, the man who was its master – when the wood behind the houses where other people lived became the *taiga* (a transformation you couldn't see or explain), Selivanov, who till then usually walked in silence, would heave a deep, joyful sigh and say, "Pity it's raining!" or "Nice weather for the time of year!", unthinkingly, but loudly and with a sense of relief, as if at last he had the right to speak out, the right of freedom.

It was a long time since he'd felt cast down if he didn't have a good day's hunting, and would fling his gun down and yell curses at his disappearing quarry. It made him laugh even to think about it now. Now, if a squirrel leapt off the branch just before he fired and fled among the trees, and his dog went rushing after it, Selivanov would smile as it disappeared. He respected it; he'd even call his dog back with a loud, shrill whistle and say, "All right, let it live, find another one! No shortage of daft ones, after all!" And even if the one that got away was valuable, the sort he needed to make his living, even that wasn't a disaster, because, after all, meeting a beast who was smarter than you was a kind of success. That was interesting, too.

Selivanov respected the *taiga* and knew in his heart that he did (the word "love" wasn't in his vocabulary), but he didn't respect other people. And all their carryings-on, the things they were up to beyond the fringes of the *taiga*, in that cramped and noisy world of theirs, well, Selivanov frankly despised all that. He thought he was lucky to have been born the way he was, and where he was, even if he hadn't had much luck with his body, what with being so small. But then this *was* a stroke of luck, because if he'd been a great hunk like Ryabinin, then surely he wouldn't have been able to resist the temptation of getting into fights all the time, surely he'd have been tempted by the power of his fists and the might of his voice? Ambition, now, that was a sin and a half – and one Ryabinin must certainly have committed.

Yes, that was right. But now here *was* Ryabinin. When Selivanov had seen him for the first time, strong and dark as an oak tree or a Siberian pine, his interest had been roused at once. An oddly passionate interest, almost like jealousy. The unfamiliar, unpleasant feeling had driven Selivanov to visit the ranger's sector more and more often, at first to commit small felonies; later it had incited him to overt provocation and rivalry, which had come to a head with Selivanov's pellet just now.

Perhaps if Selivanov had been more honest with himself, he'd have admitted that he'd been longing to have a friend for ages, someone he could tell things to and who would tell him interesting things in return. But he'd have made lots of demands on that friend; he'd have wanted him to combine many qualities which are rarely, or perhaps never, combined in a single human being. His friend had to be strong, kind, true and trusty, clever but not too keen to talk; someone capable of being close enough but not so close it got on Selivanov's nerves; the friend should need him but not depend on him, but above all he shouldn't threaten Selivanov's peace of mind – that was the main thing.

Now when his father had been alive, and they'd gone on trips into the *taiga* together, well, that had got him down. His father had been a brutal, strict man. There had been no cordiality between them, the father's power had oppressed and fettered Andrian, an only son who longed for independence and freedom, and who felt grown up very early. There was something uncaring and contemptuous in the attitude of Selivanov's father towards his sickly, skinny son. Perhaps that was why Selivanov hadn't felt particularly sorry when his father died (his mother had died a while before that). Far from appalling him, his solitude had made him happy, for, through it he had obtained his freedom, his vital rights to the *taiga* and to life, and to everything which life in the *taiga* gave him.

Ever since the time when one Nastasya, a pockmarked hussy from the village, had laughed in his face in public – he was twenty-four at the time – he'd had no idea of marrying. If he ever felt a man's desire for a woman, he would run into the *taiga*, and somehow it always seemed that the *taiga* herself would find a problem for his hunter's instincts to solve (exactly as if she sensed what was going on!) which would wear him out, until his strength was utterly exhausted, and his virility

32

as well. And later, when he was sleeping on his bunk in the hide, worn out and relaxed, he would dream of a woman, but a silent woman who had four legs and a doe's horns on her forehead, and his only desire would be to blast her away with a mighty shower of shot from both barrels.

The wise and big-hearted mastery which Selivanov's soul craved was realised in his relations with his dogs. He always had two, a dog and a bitch. Schooled in all the wisdom of the *taiga*, gentled to every domestic virtue, always well fed and well looked-after, they were his pride and joy as well as a way of making some money on the side. Their pups were worth several sable skins to the people in the villages around, and Selivanov would get orders for them two matings in advance. No matter how many pups the bitch bore, he would drown all but five, choosing the strongest and healthiest to maintain his reputation.

The time for the dogs' nuptials was a festive time for him. On the day of the mating he would take the dogs off to the furthest of his cabins. He would stay in and feed the dogs, stuffing them, but especially the male, to bursting point with meat he'd prepared in advance, and on the morning of the day when the event was to take place, he'd treat the dogs as tenderly as their own mother. It all happened before his eyes, with his approval and with his encouragement; and when the dogs, wearied and sated by their efforts, stretched out at his feet, he would stroke them and praise them and caress them, and mutter words of love to them such as only people who love each other very deeply ever say to each other, and even they not often. And if, on the day the puppies were born, the whole of mankind had been standing round the *taiga*, rows upon rows of them, and had urged him to come out and rule over all the earth – he'd have paid no heed at all! That at any rate is what Selivanov said to himself aloud, as he squatted beside the bitch in labour.

But although the whole of mankind never did come, and although no one in fact urged Selivanov to do anything, all the same, mankind did encroach on the peace of the *taiga*; it did intrude on it and torment it with its empty demands.

They'd killed his dad. Then they had a go at him too, at Andrian Nikanorych Selivanov, but they missed their chance there. He'd stood up for himself. He'd survived, and that was more than anyone else could boast. So he'd had to be fly, to cover his tracks, to pretend he was on their side, to commit a mortal sin, but nonetheless he'd got his own way by stealth and stayed as he was – on his own.

But there was no denying that over the years sadness had crept into his heart on the quiet. And it was this sadness which one day had brought the paths of Selivanov and Ryabinin together, interlacing and interweaving them.

And so now he was dragging the wounded ranger back to his chilly and unwelcoming house, digging his skis in, and he couldn't help feeling that, bad as things might seem, it was all for the best. He felt that what he was dragging back was not a disaster, but a success, almost like a quarry which he'd been dreaming of for ages, and that now his dream had come true. Selivanov wasn't taking Ryabinin's wound at all seriously. What was a tiny little hole in the leg to a hunk like that? But now they'd be bound together by their secret and by their pact.

"Freezing, are you?" he shouted out to the ranger. He turned round to speak to him but made no attempt to stop.

"Get on with it!"

"I am!" shrieked Selivanov happily.

He reckoned it would be dark by the time he got to the village; he was right, but he still made a detour round the outside of the vegetable patches just to be on the safe side. Leaving the ranger lying on the sledge, he went to open the house. He went in and lit the lamp, then returned to Ryabinin. He gasped – Ryabinin was on his feet.

"Might as well never have happened," said Ryabinin, moving a pace or two towards the porch. Selivanov darted up close to him just in case, stretching out his hands ready to catch him.

34

"Well, what did I tell you? The hole was nothing! You could have danced all night with that. You had cramp, that's all. Take care on the porch, there's a rotten board there."

Ryabinin approached the porch, still hobbling markedly, and groped his way in. As he stepped across the broad threshold, he staggered and ground his teeth. Selivanov helped him off with his snow-spattered coat and took him to the bed, where he sat him down and drew the felt boot carefully off his wounded leg. He stared into his eyes all the while and grimaced, as though feeling the pain himself. There were traces of blood on his hands.

"Started hurting again, has it? Never mind, we'll fix it good and proper this time. But lie still, now, don't try to get up!"

He opened a vast trunk with iron hoops round it which stood by the wood-burning stove, took out a piece of rag, and proceeded to tear it into bandages. Then he unbandaged Ryabinin's leg, sprinkled the wound with pine resin powder, bandaged it up again and fastened the torn trouser leg.

It was as cold inside the house as outside. The steam from their breath spread round the *izba* and was drawn like a white cloud towards the lamp, which was smoking dreadfully inside its filthy cracked globe. Selivanov flung every bit of clothing in the house on top of the wounded ranger, and then, without taking off his own outer clothing, went to busy himself with the stove. It resisted being kindled for ages, and the damp birch twigs hissed and smoked, but at length Selivanov's persistence paid off and the thing crackled into life. The *samovar* allowed itself to be lit much more easily and quickly, though it smoked even worse.

The *izba* felt unlived in because so it was. It consisted of one large room, with the Russian stove in the middle. The only other furniture was a vast bed with nickel uprights and elaborate knobs on the ends (brought from Irkutsk itself, would you believe?), a table with ribbed legs, the trunk, a bench, two stools, a home-made chest-of-drawers of crude workmanship, and the *samovar*. All this, even the *samovar*, had been left by the previous owner. In all the years he'd been there, Selivanov had brought nothing into the house. What was more, his constant absence had made the house soulless, turned it into something that was not a house at all, no more than four walls with a floor and ceiling and a row of shuttered windows.

"You live like a tramp," said Ryabinin gloomily, looking around.

"I don't live here at all," said Selivanov, not at all offended. "It's laid down officially that you have to have a house, so I've got one! You were telling me just now I don't recognise the powers that be. Well, I'm telling you there's no sense in not recognising them. It'd be as daft as trying to piss into a gale. So if they want me to be registered, I will be. That much I *can* manage!"

"The *taiga*'s one thing," said Ryabinin doubtfully, "but your own home's another! The idea of having a home wasn't thought up by them. Only a beast can live its whole life in the *taiga*."

"Well, I am a beast!" sniggered Selivanov, throwing wood on the stove, screwing his eyes up as the heat of the flame reached him and warming himself at it. "Have you ever seen a bear kill another bear? No, I haven't either. But they say in the village your dad fought in the war against his own sons. Maybe you even buried each other. So why give me this about beasts? They have their own laws. They can't go against them whether they want to or not, because their whole nature is made in terms of those laws, and you can't go against your own nature, can you? But what about a man? He and the law are two different things, and every man does his best to make his own laws. Far as I'm concerned, I'd rather they'd register me as a beast and have done."

Ryabinin smiled mockingly. "And then you'd be the king of the beasts?"

"That too!" Selivanov readily agreed.

He grabbed hold of a rusty iron ring in the floor, gave it a tug and opened the trapdoor into the cellar. He stared down for a while into the darkness, then let himself down on his elbows into the hole. For a long time he could be heard wheezing and groping about in the gloom. Then his hand appeared above the floorboards with a bottle in it, and a moment later with a jar wrapped in rags right up to its rim, then he brought out a bit of smoked bacon fat – there must have been eight pounds there at least – and only after that did Selivanov's face appear wearing a grin of pleasure. "I may not live a real life, but I never let my stores run short!"

When the house had warmed up a bit and become more cosy, they tucked into all this food, eating off the two stools shoved next to the bed. The musty *samogon* made them feel warm and even expansive. No one who'd seen them at that moment would have believed that only a few hours ago they'd been bitter enemies, that they'd shot at each other and that the blood of one of them had trickled out on to the white snow of the *taiga*. True, Ryabinin was still frowning, his voice still had an edge of ice, and now and then angry flames would flare up in his eyes, illuminated by the sooty light of the lamp. But every time Selivanov looked at him so defencelessly and innocently that the flame died down and the frost melted into a smile. And although Ryabinin intended his smile to convey mockery, to cause offence, somehow it didn't work out like that, because Selivanov eagerly received the smile as his due, he found pleasure in it, seeing in it a victory, success – and it *is* a kind of success, even a miracle, to make a friend by drawing blood from him! No plan, however well laid, to make friends with Ivan Ryabinin could have turned out like this. And now Selivanov had the happy certainty that everything had worked out: the ranger would not get away from him, he belonged to him entirely, because he was more cunning than this strong silent bull of a man and wouldn't let him go before he'd satisfied his longing for a friend.

This certainty filled Selivanov with the desire not simply to serve Ryabinin, but to be his lackey, his slave, to wash his underwear for him or to take the place of his dog and drive a wild beast out from cover for him to shoot. He was just burning with a lust to spend his last breath carrying out some wild scheme for the ranger. If Ryabinin had told him to run off to his sector and bring him a handful of snow from the roof of his cabin so that he could lick it just once, Selivanov would have run there gladly, as fast as ever he could, he could manage that, it would be a pushover for him! But Selivanov knew very well that he would always have the ranger under his thumb. He felt as if he'd gentled a powerful and noble animal into being friends with him, and now shared his power and nobility. He knew how selfish his motives were, but he felt no pangs of conscience, for he was ready to expiate them by everything he had, whether it was what God had granted him at birth or what he had acquired by good fortune since.

"I can be a lot of help to you, Vanya!" he boasted quite openly.

"I need your help like a hole in the head!" replied Ryabinin in the tone which, later, he was always to use when addressing Selivanov, and which Selivanov would accept and even encourage – it preserved the ranger's sense of security, his feeling that he was independent and superior.

"E-e-eh! Don't speak too soon! Those men in the village, for instance, they lead you by the nose. But when I show you what they're really up to, they'll squeal like stuck pigs!"

"Pooh!" Ivan sneered. "What've you got against them? What have they done to you that you want to get back at them, then?"

"No one can do anything to worry me, Vanya. But I look down on them, see. They're not even brave, they're not even cunning – they're as docile as sheep and as scared as rabbits! Just show them a horse-collar, and they'll stretch their necks out for it! They've even started to look like horses! And our present powers that be suit them down to the ground. The powers that be have got the exact measure of everyone; they know which ones'll clap to order and which ones're ready to scratch their eyes out!"

"Oh, stop blethering about the powers that be! You don't know what you're talking about. Anyway, you've no right to moan about the men in the village, you're no better than they are. What've you got to brag about?"

They were drinking blackcurrant tea and munching bits of sugar which Selivanov had chopped up with his knife. Selivanov looked longingly at the unfinished bottle of *samogon*, but the ranger showed no interest, so he had to restrain himself. And he could have downed more than one bottle this evening without getting befuddled. His experience of life had left him a lot to boast about. But boasting had always been risky, and impatience more so. Now, though, he had the *samogon* to egg him on.

"Have you seen the map, Vanya, which shows how much land they have now? No? Well, I have. I saw it in the village council! You could fit a thousand *taigas* like our one out there into it side by side. That's how much they've got their hands on! You know very well what armies fought over it, too!" Selivanov screwed up his eyes shiftily, as though he were working himself up to a desperate leap. "Arr, yes. But Chekhardak, now, Vanya, there were only three rises to stop them, but they couldn't get their hands on that, could they?"

He was holding his mug full of tea to his lips without drinking from it, and giving Ryabinin an insinuating look.

"What do you mean?"

"They couldn't get their way with it, they had to step down! And you know how they wanted to build a depot there; they rounded men up and made them go along with axes and saws. Did no good, did it?"

"Talking about the gang, are you?"

"Gang my foot, Vanya! There was no gang there! You can't call a dozen stupid village boys in horse-collars a gang, can you? It's peanuts to the powers that be! Vanya, that's their bread and butter, they love it when men get together against them, that makes them act even more daft, then they can keep them under their thumb! If they had more sense they'd make a rule that men couldn't sleep and eat in groups of less than a dozen. But one man, now, if he's got any brains . . . That's like a minnow in a stream; you can fish for it with a big net for all you're worth, but it'll still slip through!"

Ryabinin was astonished. He raised himself on to his elbows. The frown was wiped off his face, and when he twitched his bad leg he felt no pain.

"Come off it!"

Selivanov beamed.

"On your *own*?"

"Yup," Selivanov answered.

"If you're telling the truth, you know where you'll end up, doing things like that!"

Ryabinin's voice sounded more startled and disbelieving than threatening. All the same Selivanov shivered, but he couldn't stop now.

"Course I know – they'll put me up against a wall! But there's a snag, see: they have their pride too. You think they'll find it easy to believe that it was only a little squit like me standing in their way? They need proof! And where do you think they'll get that from? You should see the heaps of paper they've already used up on this: the such-and-such and so-and-so gang, and suddenly you drag me in by the scruff! And even if they accept what you say, then they won't see it as one kind of power making fun of another, they'll see it as one kind of power provoking another!"

"Selivanov, this is crap! It's just talk, you couldn't possibly have . . . on your own . . ."

As he said this, Ivan looked appraisingly at Selivanov, as if sizing him up against the events which had happened in Chekhardak, a district in the *taiga*, a few years before, and which had given rise to so many conflicting rumours amongst the locals.

Selivanov was giggling helplessly.

"Ar, you don't want to believe it, do you! Envious, aren't you! You could cripple me with just three of your big fingers, let alone your fists, couldn't you, and now you hear this! So do you think they'd believe it any easier? But now – if you were to get half the village mixed up in it, and yourself as well, then they'd give us all the chop with a clear conscience!"

"But *you*?" Ryabinin muttered, baffled.

"Honest to God, you know, if you denounced me now, then they might not believe you, but they'd come and get me anyway, just in case. But I know you'll not do that, you're not the type. I'm telling you all this hand on heart, so perhaps now you'll think different. But let's have another drop, shall we?"

"Only pigs drink after a cup of tea!" replied Ryabinin in surly tones.

Selivanov snatched a toothmarked lump of bacon off the stool and held it up close to his eyes.

"So what is a pig? Bacon, that's what! *Shpik*, the Ukrainians call it. Now listen to me, I'll hoink for you . . . Hoink, hoink . . . Ha, ha, and now I'll have another, to wash down my pig snack!"

Ivan frowned down at Selivanov hoinking, pouring himself a drink, then swilling it down amd munching his bacon with a crooked grimace. He was tormented by the fact that he couldn't get his thoughts in order, and what was more, his leg had swelled up too.

"I'll make you another cup of tea," Selivanov offered when he'd got to the end of his bit of bacon.

Ivan made no objection.

"To be really honest again, I'd never have dared do something like that if it hadn't fallen in my lap. It's really my dad I've got to thank for it." He scratched his head. "Yes, you drink that, Vanya, it's the best medicine for you now, tea is! It was like this, see. We were living in Broad Dale then, in 1920 it was. It was autumn when it happened. My dad didn't have any time for the Whites nor for the Reds either, he kept me away from them too. Let them go at each other's throats,

he says, we're for the third truth, we are. That's just what he
said – the third truth! Quite a man he was, my dad, I'll say.
Well, one day, when we were putting up new salting sheds,
far as I remember, we'd just got back to the hut when we hear
the dogs bark. No time to turn round, suddenly we've got
shooters pointed straight at us from all sides! The Whites, it
was! 'Who are you then?' they yell at us. 'Partisans, are you?
Reds?' I was bawling my eyes out and even my dad looked a
bit small. So they wanted us to show them the way to Irkutsk
so they could run off to the Mongols . . . Well, you know
yourself – follow any stream from Broad Dale, and you're
there . . . That meant they weren't locals, didn't know their
way round the *taiga* . . . Well, when dad gets control of his
tongue again he tells them, 'Any path hereabouts'll take you
straight to Irkutsk!' But suddenly this big tall one comes up
to him, with whiskers, their chief, and he looks at my father
just like a wounded elk might look, and he says, 'We must
cross the big rapids by the quickest route and before nightfall.
If you get us there . . .' and he looks round and calls a young
boy officer and says something to him. 'If you get us there,
you can have this! If you don't, I'll shoot you!'"

Selivanov got up, went to the wall and took down his gun.
"See, this is what he showed my dad, this gun. Well, dad
couldn't believe his eyes. 'We'll be there in an hour, your
honour,' he says, 'on the far side of them rapids!' The chief
poked me and said, 'This your son? Dodged the draft, has he?'
My father give him some long story. He just waves him away.
'He can go with you, and if you pull a fast one I'll shoot you
both!' We took them to the rapids by Birch Dale way. I nearly
died of fright. They're bound to blow us away, I thought, they
do that sort of thing every day! But no! We got there, and the
chief put the gun straight in my dad's hands. 'Be off with you
then!' he says. Every step of the way we were expecting a bullet
in the back, but it never came.

"It was dark when we got to the cabin. My dad spent half
the night cuddling that gun." Selivanov stroked the stock and

ran his palm along the barrel. "It's a real gent's gun! Think of the money they laid out for this, it's a disgrace! Well, my dad was caressing it so much, he seemed to know somehow he'd never get a chance to use it . . . We'd hardly woken up in the morning when we heard the dogs outside the window . . . And then the shooters in the face again. So it was the Reds. They were after the others, the Whites . . . And this time *their* chief grabs my dad by the chest, sticks his pistol against his teeth. 'Where are the Whites?' 'Don't know,' my dad answers, shaking all over. It was a daft thing to say, but he didn't know better, being the countryman he was. Their tracks were everywhere – all the officers' fancy cigarette ends. So they drag us out of doors . . . There are twice as many of them with their stars on as there were of the Whites. The chief's in leathers, he's got pop eyes and blue lips, just like a vampire. He gives my dad a shaking and swears at him. And a big hunk (bit like you) twists my arm behind my back, and he thinks I've got something to tell him too. And we knew the Whites were going to spend the night on the far side of the rapids. When I get a chance I whisper to my dad that whatever happens, one lot'll shoot us first, Whites or Reds. My dad doesn't say anything at first, then he whispers something back to me . . ." Selivanov took the gun back to its place and slopped some more *samogon* into his mug, not bothering to offer Ivan any this time. His eyes were shining and his hands shook.

"Well, you know how when you get to the last turn in Birch Dale you've got the drop on your right with the bird cherry there . . . "

Ivan nodded.

"Now, you can see the whole rapids from there. The Reds, they couldn't see anything, but me and dad could see the Whites hadn't gone. Dad jogged my elbow then, and we signalled to them from the top of the drop. Lordy, Vanya, when my ski got stuck on the twig and I went arse over tip in the snow, and you were behind me . . . That was the second time in my life I'd felt like that . . . Well, my dad ran down

43

to the bottom without making a sound, and when they'd already got away, fancy, my dad suddenly yells, 'Fire! Fire!' I belted down to him. And he was on his knees and shouting, clutching the gun they'd given him. Then down he went. The bullet'd gone in between his shoulder blades. So I dragged him back to the rises to avoid Birch Dale. And all those miles I dragged him, right to Larch Dale. We had another bloody cabin there, see, him and me. I buried him there . . ." Selivanov was silent, squinting at the lamp with melancholy eyes. "No bloody light at all from that. Whole globe's covered in soot. So. Well, I sold my dad's house, but you don't want to hear about that, it's got nothing to do with the story. Then the co-operative got on my tail. And then they decided to build the depot here. And some bastard has to say it should be in Chekhardak. Wish I'd . . ."

"Bastard yourself!" Ryabinin snarled. "I said it. It was the best place for it."

Selivanov opened his eyes wide.

"You!"

"Yes, me! Well, if we're going to do the job properly, Chekhardak couldn't be better! And I'm not sorry I said it!"

"You!" Selivanov gasped again. "Do the job properly! What sort of job is that, Vanya, mucking up the *taiga*?"

"We don't have to muck it up! We have to have food stores in the *taiga*, so we don't have to travel to fetch it in winter."

"Eeh, Vanya!" Selivanov shook his head. "You're only three years younger than me, but you might be ten, on brains."

"Good job you're so damn clever, then!"

"Did you have a look what they were building there?"

"Not my job to look, is it? Well, I did go down, at the beginning, when they were looking for where to build it . . ."

"Don't you believe in God, Vanya? I don't much either, but sometimes I think he really is there. If I'd known then it was you said it . . . Wouldn't do any harm to cross myself!" Rolling his eyes, Selivanov crossed himself and shook his head sadly. "Well, they rounded up some of their tame village men, the cart-horses. I won't tell you all the foul things they got up to, so as not to plague your conscience; after all, my sin cancelled out yours, and more . . ."

"Leave my conscience alone, you'd best be rummaging in your own, I bet what's there's as black as the hair on your head!"

Ryabinin twisted round, trying to change position. Selivanov scuttled up to him and started to shift him carefully and deftly.

"Is your leg swollen?"

"A bit."

Selivanov plumped up a pillow and laid it under Ivan's head, then took his jacket off the nail, felt to see if it was wet, and put that under his head too. Ivan flopped back on to the bedhead and gestured at Selivanov to stop fussing. Selivanov lay down on the bench with his hands under his head.

"Well then. The place you showed them was where I had my best runs of goats . . . And a mile or so away there was one of my cabins, the best I had! So the men arrived. There was one of them had blubber lips and steel teeth, and was tattooed with all sorts of crap all over, from his arse to his chin . . . Well, so I made out I'd been chosen to be the watchman from the co-operative. But actually I'd come over from the other side of Chekhardak, from Atamanikha. Anyway, after I sold my house I hadn't lived anywhere at all, I was in the *taiga* winter and summer. Except I'd go and see this woman maybe twice a season. And when they formed the co-op in Luchikha and gave it rights in the *taiga*, I turned up there as if I was a completely new arrival, and as if it was just coincidence I asked to work on the depot. So they made me watchman, see. Right, so the one with the tattoos and the mouth full of iron, he made me cook their grub . . . More or less kicked me in the backside, come to that. But never mind that! We'd start a bonfire in the evening, sing a few dirty songs at the tops of our voices, and then he'd get us all round the bonfire and tell us to piss on it to put it out! Vanya, would you have stood for it? Listen to this, too. If he ever found a tree with an anthill ⁻

under, then he'd tell us to chop the tree down, and then he'd climb on the stump and shit on the anthill. When he saw the ants die from his filth, he'd piss himself laughing! And then, Vanya, he decided to do something to me I can't even tell you about! If he *had* done it, I tell you, I'd have hanged myself the very next morning!

"So I ran away that evening to Birch Dale, got hold of a viper there – that's the only place you'll find them hereabouts – and put it on him while he was lying snoring on the moss. It bit him in the arm just above the elbow. By next morning he'd had it. The men all took fright and bolted out of the *taiga*. I was rejoicing, but then two days later they all came back and they had a new chief . . . Who do you think he was? It was that same man who was the chief of the Reds when they made my dad and me show them the path. Course, I was only a little lad then, but he had sharp eyes. He gave me a few funny looks . . . That was when I realised I had to go. But where could I go, away from my own home?

"Then later some more men came and joined him, not country men like the others, but some of the new lot, so far as I could see. With guns. They started to blast the place apart. They shot anything that moved, and they kept on hanging round my cabin. Well, Vanya, that was when I vowed it would be war to the death, with no quarter." Selivanov said this last sentence in a solemn tone, but immediately grinned maliciously. "For them, that is, 'cos they weren't men enough to finish me off! And so, Vanya, now I'll tell you my big secret." Selivanov got up off the bench, perched closer to Ryabinin, bent down to him and said, almost whispering. "If you stand with your back to that building they'd started work on, do you remember what you see?"

"A hill, I think . . ."

"Egsakly! And if you go up the path from the depot to where you leave the *taiga*, which way does the path turn? Remember?"

"Right, I'd say . . ."

Selivanov grinned with pleasure. Ryabinin was annoyed, but he didn't let it show; the story was interesting.

"And if you go five miles or so from the depot, what will you have on the left?"

Ryabinin answered, without hesitating this time, "A cliff, of course!"

"Your memory's worth its weight in gold, Vanya! A cliff, for sure! But which one?"

"What are you pestering me for? Any old one, get to the point!"

"But that is the point! It's the same cliff as the hill outside the depot!"

"What are you on about?" Ryabinin snorted.

Selivanov beamed as brightly as the side of the *samovar* where the light fell on it.

"The beauty of it is, the path from the depot turns sharp right but then, 'cos there've been stone falls in a couple of places, it goes in a bit towards the left, a pace or so, sometimes less, but it goes in for the whole five miles! So the upshot is, the path bends back on itself and goes round behind the hill where it looks like a cliff! My dad let me into the secret. So, when you want to get out of the *taiga* in a hurry, you can do it four times quicker as the crow flies. It's damn steep, especially from the top down to the path; but it's fast! When that hole in your leg heals up, I'll show you!" Selivanov thumped his knees delightedly. "So what did I do, Vanya? My dad thought of everything. He had an old rifle and a couple of cartridge belts from the Civil War hidden up on Bald Hill. They used to wear those belts cross-wise over their belly buttons, the squaddies did. Bald Hill's a long way off, but so what. I tore off up there and got the rifle and hid it at the top of the cliff. Then I built myself a shack with its back wall into the hill, so I could crawl in there on the sly if I needed to. So what then? I waited! When the heroes had had enough of their shooting, they loaded the meat on to their horses. I helped them tie it on myself. And before they left, I decided to

47

give the horses some water so they wouldn't get thirsty, the sweethearts! Well, I stepped back . . ." Selivanov narrowed his eyes knowingly, "and fell straight in the stream with all my clothes on! The shooting party had a good laugh at me and then they were off, and our chief went with them to show them the way. When they'd left, I took off all my clothes in front of everyone, hung them on the bushes, and went into the shack in my knickers, saying I was going to have a snooze. But I went out through the back wall and belted up through the thicket to the top of the hill. Went up as though I was on wings, and when I got there I had to wait some more! Nearly caught my death. I looked down – there they were, coming along, hands on hips, tongues wagging. I crouched down – it was quite far away, a hundred and fifty paces or so in a straight line – and as soon as the hero in leathers shows me his chest, I blow him away! You should have seen him fly out of the saddle like a sack of dung, Vanya! I put the rifle in its hiding place and was off downhill! Got scratched to blazes, though! I crept out of the hut, shivering like mad, and got into my damp clothes, went to help the men with their work . . . An hour later they turned up with the body! Well, that was how it started. One chief after another would arrive, each one more horrible than the last, start sniffing round and swaggering about the *taiga* with his cronies, and when they were on the way home I'd get up the hill and – bang! Right up to the very top one of all! Then, if you remember, they sent a whole detachment, they combed the whole *taiga*, and when they were leaving I got the chief again!"

Selivanov burst into peals of laughter. Ryabinin looked at him wide-eyed, as though Selivanov had gone mad.

"But that last one, that's the only time I screwed it up a bit, I only blew his hand off, so now he's serving as a judge in Slyudyanka . . . And so what then? So they closed the depot, Vanya! I was worried at first they'd change the site to Ledy-anka, that's only a stone's throw away from Chekhardak, after all! But there's been not a whisker of them there. True, afterwards they sent a detachment or two in, and I think I may have heard a rumour they caught someone. But I didn't lay a finger on them . . . So that's my story, Vanya, every word true! Going to tell on me, are you?"

Selivanov's question had an edge of anxiety, though he was still beaming with the joy his confession had roused in him.

"You're a deep one!" Ryabinin spat out in a surly tone, although his voice also held something very close to respect, or maybe he felt fear of this little man whom only an hour ago he'd taken for a pushover. "As the rules are I should nab you now, because you're an enemy of the powers that be."

"No, Vanya," Selivanov broke in. "It's *my taiga*, and yours, and the others', and our justice is the third kind, the one between theirs. I didn't run to them with my justice, I didn't go against their law. What does their law say? It's all supposed to be for the peasants! But what has any peasant ever got out of their justice!"

"How come you've started going on about the peasants all of a sudden? You want to do them down yourself!" said Ryabinin savagely.

"Don't take everything I say so seriously! I'm fed up with the peasants because they behave like harness horses! If they'd only take it into their heads to be fiercer, they'd have every government eating out of their hand! Isn't that so?"

"But if everyone's going to run things . . ."

"Pooh!" Selivanov waved this away. "Say I'm walking in the *taiga* and I stop to look at a pine thicket, and I can see a birch sapling growing there, and at the end of the summer all I can see is a dried-up stick! Why? Because a pine thicket isn't the right place for a birch sapling! That's not in any rules, it just happens all by itself. And if peasants are allowed to live by themselves, then the laws will grow up by themselves too! I'm not s'posed to go into your salting sheds and that's it! That's the law! Who made it? No one! So since when has it been like that? Bet even my grandad couldn't have told you! If you build a house, you won't cut down a tree so it'll fall on my house,

49

will you? No, you won't even think of it! That's the law! And we don't need these people all covered in stars with revolvers stuck on their bellies to make us stick to it! And if there's any law which can't be kept without a revolver to make people keep it, then that means it's flying in the face of everyone, except the revolver! Vanya, do you think it was mischief or wickedness made me take out those swine with their stars on when I was on the cliff? If you really want to know, I racked my brains to jelly every time so I could understand my own justice clearly!"

"You're a killer, that's your only truth, your only justice!"

Selivanov seemed to reach the point of desperation. He was not talking now, he was shouting. He'd started pacing round the room. As the bench was in his way, he had to step over it each time he crossed from corner to corner.

Ryabinin had propped himself against the head of the bed. He looked morose, but his expression was also one of worry and distress.

"Why am I a killer?" Selivanov shouted. "So what did they all do in the war?" – he waved his hand – "kill rabbits, or what? Nobody calls them killers! The ones who killed the most got all the power and glory!"

"Fool!" Ivan lashed out. "That was the war!"

"So I'm a fool?" In his fury Selivanov jerked his head as if complaining to someone or other hidden behind the stove. "Why do wars happen, then? One tsar cheats another at cards, so the other smears snot on his shirt front, tit for tat! And then they go and send their soldiers off to fight each other. The soldiers tear the guts out of each other, and the tsar who's left without any soldiers is the loser. That's all there is to it!"

"You really are a fool!" Ryabinin repeated. "In the last war the people were fighting for justice, against the tsar, and you went and hid in the *taiga*!"

"No, you're the fool!" Selivanov darted up to him. "Your father fought against your own brothers! What sort of justice is that, for a father to fight against his own sons?"

50

"Leave my family out of this, you bastard, or I'll smash your face in!"

Ryabinin had half-risen and clenched his fists. He was about to leap off the bed.

"Go on, smash it in, then!" shouted Selivanov, his voice rising almost to a squeal. He kicked the bench aside so it wouldn't get in the way. The bench overturned, taking the two stools with it, and the bottle with the remains of the *samogon* smashed to smithereens. The mugs jangled along the floor, rolling over and over. "Why do you want to hit me? Because of what I said about justice?" Selivanov looked like a little terrier which had fastened on a bull with its small sharp teeth. "All right, so my sort of justice isn't too clean! But where's yours? What is it? I blew the star-spangled bastards away from the cliff because I'd declared war on them, because they'd shat on my justice! I had the right to declare war on them too! And everyone has the right to if he's not allowed to live! A killer is someone who kills in order to get his hands on other people's property! But I did it to protect my own! What have the peasants got out of the justice they smashed each other's skulls in to get?"

"There's one thing I do know," said Ryabinin, drawing back; "you're an enemy of the powers that be, and I want nothing to do with you!"

"Just look what he's got into his head!" Selivanov threw up his hands in despair. "I'm not their enemy! They're *my* enemy!"

Ryabinin turned his back in silence and didn't say another word. Selivanov paced about the *izba* for a bit longer, then lay down to sleep, sighing and wheezing.

The next morning Selivanov woke before it was light. He lit the fire and brought fresh water from the well, got the *samovar* going and tidied up the *izba*. While he was doing all this he kept an eye on the sleeping ranger. When Ivan stirred and woke up, he asked him how his leg was. He rebandaged it, enthusing over the way the blood had clotted cleanly on the wounds, and gave Ivan some tea to drink.

Ivan sat silent for some time. Then, as if by chance, his glance fell on Selivanov's rifle hanging on its nail by the door.

"Fine piece!" said Ryabinin, coughed, and added loudly, "Er, by the way, I didn't hear any of that last night!"

"Good!" Selivanov responded happily. "We had a few glasses of *samogon* last night. It's terrible stuff, makes you say God knows what! That's the end of the story! Lie down. I'm going to have a look at the dogs. I didn't go and get them yesterday, and they've been next door with my neighbours' lot for a week. They'll need fattening up, I'll be bound!"

So that's how it was. Only it wasn't the end of the story, the story was only just beginning . . .

THREE

And if Selivanov, now an old man sitting on his birch log near what was once the Ryabinin house, had recalled the past in all its details and in proper sequence, as narrated above, he too might have said that, "the story was just beginning".

But he remembered nothing at this late hour, though doubtless his thoughts were about the past, and that past was in some sense a recollection. It is possible that certain scenes became visible to his consciousness, certain voices could be heard – his own voice too, which he had disliked all his life because of its uncontrollable tendency to yelp. Perhaps, though, he heard and saw nothing at all and simply couldn't bring himself to draw nearer to the threshold of the Ryabinin house. While he dragged his feet he thought about other things or about nothing at all, as only old men know how . . .

It was in . . . well, the year doesn't matter. It was midsummer, the best time of year, the emptiest for the hunter. Selivanov pined for whole days on end, and, in order to give himself something to do, rushed about the *taiga* with Ivan Ryabinin for the hell of it, chasing off poachers with guns and casual strangers who could have scared a capercaillie hen hiding her young amongst the bilberries, or picked off the hazel-hen chicks which were perched like carrot-tops on the birch branches. He took salt to the hunters' salting-sheds, cut hay for the deer and set his cabin to rights.

One day, when he'd been hanging around Chekhardak the

best part of a week, he reached the point where his ribs, and his dogs' ribs, were sticking out like a toast-rack. Towards noon, in the heat of the day, he dragged himself to Ryabinovka and, without further ado, staggered into the village store.

On his way there, he caught sight of an unfamiliar figure over by the fence. Something about it drew his eye even then; it wasn't foreboding exactly, but his gaze was somehow arrested by the man instead of glancing off him.

In the shop he had a good gossip with the girl behind the counter, gathered food into his knapsack, had a snack and tossed something to the dogs which had burst in with him. Then he started to brag about his dogs to the men hanging round there with nothing to do. An hour passed, more. Had he forgotten the man? Indeed he had. But as he left, he shot a look over to the fence, and now his heart missed a beat. There were two of them now, the first one and a lanky, sour-looking lad. They looked straight at Selivanov, quite openly, though who could tell what the stares were for? He went up to the Ryabinin house, glancing back at least a dozen times, but no, they hadn't come after him. But they had certainly been looking at him. And Selivanov had an idea that there was something familiar about the face of one of them . . . maybe both . . .

Fear struck him behind the knees, and his legs buckled. He wished to God Ivan were home; with Ivan not even the devil himself could frighten him . . .

When he was still at the gate, he could see that the house was locked up, and he had another look round. He didn't open the door, but ran stumbling to the barn, found a chain and some rope and used it to tie the dogs to the porch. Fat lot of use that was! They were worthless as watchdogs. They might make a timid man pause a bit, but someone who knew dogs would just pat them on the flank and carry on. Hunting dogs. They could guard a forest cabin, but they didn't know the value of a house, it was all the same to them whichever fence you tied them to.

When Selivanov reached the porch, he stretched up on tip-toe and looked out through the wicker fence at the road from the village. Only then did he turn the lock. He went straight in, shooting the bolt on the hall door. The inner door didn't have a bolt; but anyway, at that moment it came to him that if the men wanted to get even with him over some hunting business or other, they would hardly come into the house; no, they'd lie in wait in the dark or watch out along the *taiga* road. Disaster averted! He'd wait for Ivan and not show his nose till he got back.

The shutters were closed, but cracks let in light and even sunshine on the south side. After watching for a while, he went to the living quarters and lit a lamp, then reloaded the gun with buckshot in both barrels. Finally he sat down on a stool, whisking his cap off his head and into the corner.

There was something still gnawing at Selivanov, he was uneasy, feeling there was something important he'd overlooked . . . And what if it was the Cheka! What if they'd made enquiries about his doings at Chekhardak! Yes, that pair hadn't really looked anything like peasants, there was something military about them . . . And the boots on them, he suddenly remembered, sort of ordinary at first glance, but, then again, they'd been ever so straight over the calves – ever so tight-fitting. And was that a service jacket peeking out from under that man's padded coat?

This was far worse than if it was simply one of the men from the village out for revenge! What's more, Ivan wouldn't be able to stand up for Selivanov, would he, not if they were going to put the squeeze on him, Ivan could hardly help opening his mouth then, could he? So what was he to do? Make for the *taiga* at top speed, and avoiding the path!

He started pacing about the house, sighing and groaning; he even got a fit of the hiccups. He looked for his cap, found it at length, then unloaded and reloaded the gun. Pulling up the trapdoor to the cellar, he grabbed half a flitch of fat bacon and a few jars of preserves. He leapt up again like a hare, rummaged in the sideboard, scrabbling the entire contents out into his knapsack, tied it shut and slung it over his shoulder.

He went into the hall, taking care the inner door didn't squeak, and stared long and hard through the opening in the hall door. There was no one to be seen, so he stuck his head out. The dogs were pacing about the porch; they jumped up and started whining. As he shut the door, hid the key, untied the dogs, he kept glancing about, and began to calm down a little. He was right – he should leave directly, search for Ivan in the *taiga* and find out from him what was what.

The dogs flew joyfully out of the gate. Then, as Selivanov shut it, he heard footsteps and a voice.

"Andrei Nikanorych, if I am not mistaken?"

It was one of the two, and yes, no doubt about it, that *was* a service jacket peeking out from his coat – rather a shabby one, it was true.

Let him have it with both barrels, then run for it! was Selivanov's first thought, but the next one sobered him up: he'd never get the gun off his shoulder in time! "Now I'm done for!" he moaned to himself, and feigned a fit of coughing to play for time before speaking.

The dogs had taken a turn around the nearest rowan. Now they came back and started milling round the men's legs. The stranger looked sideways at them mistrustfully and asked, "Don't bite, do they?"

Not a Chekist! – Selivanov breathed relief. A frightened Chekist wouldn't stand there asking fool questions, he'd shoot. And no country man, either! Even the daftest country man knows his dogs.

"What else did God give them mouths for?" he answered the stranger, looking at him more calmly now, but then he spied a hand movement which you could never mistake: the man had a revolver inside his jacket. All the same, not a Chekist! That was for sure. And what was more, he was no more than a young lad. Hadn't noticed that at first, he'd had such a miserable look on his face. Still only a kid!

"I've some business with you, Andrei Nikanorych . . ."

Selivanov gave a cough and replied, not without a certain hauteur:

"I am not named Andrei. On the day of my appearance in the world, that was not the saint in the church calendar, but Andrian, so it's he I'm named for. It may be a daft name, but it's mine. So, what is this business you have with me?"

Oh, how bold he'd got, even addressing the man with the familiar form, smiling to himself at his recent fears! And what if the man did have a revolver by his side? Wouldn't be the first time Selivanov had seen the likes of that in all these years!

"A certain person wants a word with you . . . We'll go to him now."

"If somebody needs me, he can come here himself," Selivanov began to say, but suddenly everything changed. Whilst the man was standing three or four paces away – even when he was at arm's length – he was just a man; but then suddenly he stepped right up to Selivanov and turned out to be a good head taller. His face had changed, too, as though a mask had slipped. As always in such circumstances, Selivanov immediately felt small and pitiable, and he gave in, as he always did in the face of the big or the bold.

"I don't give a damn what they call you, got it!" the stranger enunciated clearly and distinctly through clenched teeth. "I was told to go and fetch you, and fetch you I will, if I have to wrap that shotgun round your neck!"

Shrinking into himself, Selivanov thought first sadly of Ivan, then angrily of the dogs – just look at them gambolling underfoot, no sense in them! He asked submissively, "Where are we headed for?"

Although the gesture which the stranger made with his hand was quite vague, Selivanov guessed they were going by the lower rowan thicket, round the outside of the village, to somewhere at its far end. If it was Ivan, he'd have been grinning on the other side of his face! he thought while moving. Or the dogs – if you could just tell them, "fetch!", and one of them grabbed him by the throat and the other by the arse! Then this hero here'd be in a fine pickle, heh! What if I did manage to get one shot in?

But Selivanov himself knew it was futile – it would never work. He was still hoping nothing awful would happen. Who needed him? He'd already guessed. So the star-spangled scum hadn't put paid to all of the other lot yet, then? But there wasn't much joy in this thought either. What was the use? How weak is a bullet fired against the powers that be, how strong is one fired in their defence! But fine fellows like this couldn't work that out, could they, they would go running round and getting carved up without a hope of victory or glory, just making trouble for other people. And what had all this to do with him, anyway? He lived by his own lights, for himself. That was how it'd been all his life: it was hard enough for anyone to grab hold of him, and in any case he was no slouch, he could stand up for himself if he wanted to!

But just at that moment Selivanov, so to speak, put his hand on the wriggling tail of a tiny worm of disquiet which had shoved its revolting snout through his self-confidence.

What if it was a Chekist who had him by the scruff of the neck? He'd guessed as much from the start. It'd been at the back of his mind, he just hadn't allowed the thought to take shape. Had God got something up his sleeve for him, Selivanov, too? Was there maybe some misery meant for him hatching out of its rotten egg somewhere? At the very least, who could guarantee there wasn't a fallen tree lying in wait for him along a path somewhere, ready to break his legs?

All this time they had been crossing the lower rowan stand and skirting the village, and the man behind didn't once speak to Selivanov, not even to tell him whether to go right or left. So where was he being taken? In his mind, he went through every house at that end of the village and decided that it had to be Svetlichnaya's they were going to. It stood in the heart of a stand of rowans, a bit to the side and away from the road. That poxy hag! thought Selivanov, not without a touch of respect for the woman. And, strangely, he now felt for her as an ally, though he'd never thought of her in that light before.

So Selivanov confidently turned left and went about fifty paces in that direction. Suddenly his collar was caught in a grip so hard the shirt dug into his throat.

"How do you know where we're going?"

Selivanov started to wheeze (pretending, of course). When he was freed, he fell to the ground, clutching his throat and rolling his eyes.

"What's up with you?" the man asked in alarm, and bent down beside him.

"You've broken my neck, you clodhopping brute!" wheezed Selivanov, rolling his eyes up to his brow. "Give me water, quick, or I'll peg out this minute!"

"Water?" the man's head began to spin.

Oh, Selivanov knew this well, this irrepressible daring of his that would well up in his puny body as if from nowhere! How he would shake inwardly at the risk he was taking, yet needs have to follow where the impulse led him, for it was stronger than any liquor which another man might pour down his throat to give him Dutch courage.

"Water!" he croaked. "There's a spring there – over by the bushes."

The lanky lad rushed off.

"Hands up!" screeched Selivanov that instant, already on his feet, gun cocked. "Hands up, pig shit, or I'll blow you to smithereens!"

But why had he done it? Five minutes back and he'd had no idea of doing anything of the sort. It had come of its own accord. His legs quivered like a sheep's at slaughter, his heart beat wildly.

The man's mouth twisted, but he raised his hands a little way in the air, and looked twice as tall. Teeth bared, and the look in his eyes – God preserve us!

Maybe I should blow him away once and for all? the idea popped into Selivanov's head. But they'll find him here: they'll eventually have found it, no way round it! Curiosity about the whole business still gnawed at him. Who needed him, and why?

"What were your orders? Fetch me, right? And did they tell you to grab me by the throat and choke me too?"

The man stood breathing malice, obviously looking for a way to break free. His pupils were black as night and glared such determination that Selivanov realised he must either shoot him at once or try another tack.

"We weren't born yesterday, either!" he said boastfully, pleased with himself now. "See, the way I looked at it, if someone needs me, by rights I should go! But as for where, my lad, well that don't take much reckoning. Svetlichnaya's the only one lives out here, all on her own, and the path to her place through this patch of rowans is the quietest by a long way."

Selivanov continued in this boisterous tone, though he felt really wobbly at the knees: "Look here, dickhead! Get that look out of your eyes! I was joking. Don't reach for your shooter, you won't be needing it!"

He lowered the gun, the man lowered his hands.

"Shall we get going?"

And now once more Selivanov had turned into a wretched little fellow, and he knew it. The transformation stifled, or almost stifled, the tall man's rage. You could see he was not himself yet, but he managed to hiss, "I'll teach you to play jokes like that on me!"

"So how would you like to be grabbed by the throat?" Selivanov whined pitifully, flinging his gun over his shoulder.

"Enough said! Let's go!"

Selivanov wiped the sweat from his brow. His opponent mechanically did the same.

"You're one to watch, that's for sure," the man said with mingled malice and disbelief. "Nothing to look at, but you jumped me."

Before they'd even reached the kitchen garden, Svetlich-naya's russet-coloured dog broke out barking. Selivanov's dogs scampered off round the fence, but when the men got up to the porch, the kennel turned out to be empty. The old woman had tied the dog up to the barn. He was dead vicious, that dog of hers, and she was afraid he might bite her guests. Svetlichnaya herself met them in the hall and, seeing Selivanov, clapped her hands together in feigned surprise.

"Well, if it isn't Andrian Nikanorych!"

"That's right. I've come to propose to you!" Selivanov replied in a spiteful tone, as he took off his cap and pulled off his boots.

"And I would be glad to accept your offer!" cried Svetlich-naya, keening. "Who wouldn't jump at you! As a hunter, no one can touch you. And I'd give you every loving care, you can be sure of that. But how can I think of it, poor miserable woman that I am?"

As she gave voice to all this, a thought suddenly struck Selivanov between the eyes: perhaps he could propose for real. Then he was brought to his senses by a light tap on the shoulder, and, shuffling his feet again, he went into the room.

On the bed, covered to his throat with a quilted blanket, lay the second man. At his feet sat a girl about nineteen years old, white-skinned and golden-haired, with a long plait to her waist. The sight of her arrested Selivanov's gaze. He hadn't expected to see such a marvel, something so far beyond the ken of village life. After a closer look, he guessed she was the daughter of the man who was lying on the bed sick; his cheeks and brow burned with fever and his eyes had an unhealthy glow.

"Sit down, please, Andrian Nikanorych! Take a seat and come close!"

The sick man spoke in a quiet, hoarse voice. By his manner Selivanov reckoned straight off that what he had before him was one of the "ex-s". An officer, no doubt about it! He took a chair from by the window and sat on it, placing the gun between his knees and covering the barrel with his cap.

The man who'd brought him was standing in the passage, elbows up against the door jamb, not speaking. A subordinate, then. The old woman had stayed in the hall.

"My name is Nikolai Aleksandrovich."

Selivanov got to his feet, all polite.

"And this is my daughter, Lyuda . . . Lyudmila."

The girl looked at Selivanov quietly and seriously and from her look he understood that they both needed him very much.

"You don't recognise me, then?" the sick man said suddenly, gazing not at Selivanov, but at the gun.

Selivanov stopped short.

"In the shop . . . eeh . . . thought I recognised you, sir . . ."

"So you did notice. Your father, by the way . . . they told me . . . he's died, has he?"

Selivanov decided not to touch on that subject and mumbled diplomatically, "May he rest in peace . . ."

"Your father had that gun from my own hands!"

Selivanov first screwed his eyes shut, then fearfully lowered them.

"Have you nothing to say?"

"I remember the man my dad had this gun off, even though I was only a mite then, so, I mean to say, beg pardon for saying so sir, but there must be some mistake here."

The sick man raised himself very slightly; the daughter straightened his blanket at once and plumped the pillow a little higher.

"Colonel Bakhmetev presented the gun to your father, but it was mine to give. I was a second lieutenant then."

Yes, for sure, Selivanov could remember that young officer hovering about the colonel. So, the face really was familiar.

"Hem. You didn't get away that time, then?" he asked carefully. Although how was the officer to know what Selivanov knew, how he and his father had brought the Reds on them?

"We got away. There was a fight, but we got away. My daughter . . ."

He looked at the girl, she answered his look, and there was

62

a "something" in this exchange of glances, a hint of the love between father and daughter, though Selivanov could only guess at this, because no one in the world had ever looked at him like that.

Again the thought flashed through his mind: should he propose to Svetlichnaya? All right, she was a bit long in the tooth, but there could still be a child . . . and, God willing, a lassie too. Maybe he'd be spared till she could look at him like that. Oh Lord! The very thought was enough to make you die of joy!

"My daughter stayed behind at my house in Irkutsk, she was only a year old."

Once more they looked at each other, their eyes moistening just visibly.

"So then I returned . . . to see my daughter for myself."

– What did he mean by that, returned? – Selivanov was confused. Where from? Where did he come back from, to see his daughter? Better keep a weather eye! Something here smelt fishy, the stink could turn your nostrils inside out! –

"Well then, to see your daughter for yourself . . ." Selivanov repeated, as though he was a bit soft in the head.

"Semyon, Lyudochka, please sit out on the porch while we talk . . ."

The imploring tone seemed to be addressed more to the lanky lad than to the girl. She plumped the pillow once more, and rose dutifully. The man eagerly (Selivanov made a mental note of this eagerness) stepped up to her and put his hand out in lordly style, leering all over his face. But she stepped past without taking his hand, and this Selivanov noted too, though he was pretending to be looking the other way. In the hall, after the door had slammed behind them, Svetlichnaya gave a cough, reminding them of her presence, but the officer paid not the slightest attention, and this meant that the woman must be fully in his confidence. Svetlichnaya's worth in Selivanov's eyes went up threefold.

The officer looked him in the eye. There was nothing

guarded or suspicious there, he was simply trying to make his man out, at least as far as it's possible to make someone out from his face. Selivanov couldn't bear those eyes looking at him, because he'd never been able to hold anyone's stare. He knew that this weakness did him no good at all, but the leopard can't change his spots, can he?

"What kind of man are you, Selivanov? I know next to nothing of you, but I do know that Yuliana Feodorovna Svetlichnaya speaks well of you . . . So I thought I'd risk it."

I'll marry her, Selivanov had now made up his mind.

"Do you acknowledge the new powers? I mean, in your heart?"

"What other power is there?" Selivanov answered carefully.

The officer heaved a weary sigh.

"You're cunning enough, I can see that. But since I have no other way out, I'll be frank with you. If you betray me, let God be your judge! But if you say anything to my daughter about this conversation . . ."

Selivanov understood from the look which flared up for an instant in the man's eyes that truly all this was because of her, all that the man wanted to say about himself.

"I'm sick. Consumption. D'you know what that is?"

"Not really!" Selivanov exclaimed, looking at him again, straight in the eye.

"I won't hold out till autumn . . ."

Selivanov wanted to make some objection, it was impossible not to when you heard things like that, but the other man held him back with a gesture. He wanted neither condolences nor consolation.

"When I found out, I was filled with horror at the idea of dying in a strange country. I got hold of some people, other Russians, who had business in Russia. I persuaded them to send me. I didn't expect to get through. Not many make it . . . But I'm here, as you see. I travelled to Siberia to look for my daughter, but time was getting short, there wasn't enough to see the thing through. I wanted to spend my last days with my

64

daughter. But where? I remembered your father. Suddenly I wondered, was he still alive? He helped us once before! Now here you are . . . can you hide us in the forest? It's not for long. My word as an officer. My daughter knows I've come from over there but she doesn't know about the illness, thinks I've got a cold." He was silent.

"Here I am, a former officer, a nobleman, appealing to you, a Russian peasant . . . if you are still a true Russian, that is: let me die a free man. I can repay you with nothing but trouble, and maybe even danger too."

The officer certainly knew how to talk to a man. Selivanov was almost unbearably moved, and could say nothing to begin with, though he absolutely had to reply. But he only fidgeted restlessly on his chair, describing incomprehensible gestures in the air with his hands. He was filled with joyful readiness to service the man, and the thought that, when all was said and done, the business was dangerous, didn't once enter his mind.

"Eh, well now . . ." he found his tongue at last. "The *taiga* – now put it this way, we're the bosses here! And what's all this about dying! I'll have you on your feet in less than a week! I've all the roots and herbs to cure you!"

The sick man smiled wanly.

"Mother Nature herself has no remedy for my sickness, or if there is one, men have yet to find it . . . So, will you hide us?"

"Course I will! Only, sir, how'll you manage to get there? To be safe, we must go a long way in . . ."

"Couldn't we have a horse . . . ?"

Selivanov slapped his knee in annoyance.

"What a twit I am! Of course! We'll find a pony and a saddle for you."

"Forgive me," the officer interrupted him, "but would two be out of the question?"

"Well, that young ox is sturdy enough. He can get there on his own two feet."

"I meant my daughter . . ."

Selivanov grimaced again, raging at his own lack of understanding. "Fair enough. Two'll be harder, but we'll do it somehow. But can she cope in the saddle?"

"If we don't go flat out . . ."

"Surely," agreed Selivanov and finally let himself ask the question which had been on the tip of his tongue. "And Lanky there, who might he be, if you don't mind me asking, of course? So that I know . . . well . . . how to . . . with him."

The other man's face darkened noticeably and he cast a glance at the door, pondering his reply, hoping perhaps that Selivanov would drop the question. Selivanov, however, set his face as though he hadn't understood the embarrassment and silence. He stared like an idiot, as only he knew how, at the officer.

"He'll be with me a while . . . and then . . . he'll go. If it should occur to you to betray him, kindly bear in mind that I advise you most strongly against it."

Hey . . . Selivanov weighed this up. It's not so straightforward as I thought: which of the two *is* the boss here? Better keep a weather-eye open.

"In that case, then," he got up and slung the gun on his shoulder, "I'll go for the horse – no sooner said than done. And you'll be ready, then? I think we'll be moving along tomorrow morning early . . ."

At this point the officer was seized by a fit of coughing such as Selivanov had never heard before, and he understood by some queer foreboding that this man was a goner, not of this world. Quietly, he sidled out of the door.

Lyudmila and Lanky were sitting on the top step of the porch. Both stood up as soon as they saw Selivanov. Lyudmila slipped back through the door right away, and Selivanov found Lanky blocking his path. Selivanov realised that he couldn't get past, so he had to crane his neck to look up at the man.

"Well, so what did you agree on?" Lanky asked, looking at him in none too friendly a fashion.

"What needs to be done! And I'll do it. 'Scuse me now, me lad, time's short and there's still plenty to do."

With these words he made to slip away from the porch but his shoulder was caught in an iron grip.

"Watch yourself, no jokes!"

Selivanov's tongue quivered in his mouth with the urge to say something sharp to the young man, but his brains curbed his tongue – quite right too, that's what it's for, after all.

Assuming an expression of boundless submissiveness and selflessness, hunching himself still lower, and making himself look even more puny and unprepossessing, Selivanov whimpered:

"Can't see why you're taking on so. My dear sir, doubt me not."

That "doubt me not," which Selivanov would never in a hundred years have used in earnest, he let out now on purpose, since he knew the force of a servile intonation. Nothing could get through better to big strong thickies like this. No, clearly Lanky hadn't forgotten his "joke" in the forest, for now he shook Selivanov by the shoulder, almost knocking him off the porch. Only nimble footwork prevented him from teetering off the steps.

Selivanov wasn't sure he could keep up the act so, without turning round, he minced past the house and belted through the wicket gate. Passing beyond where he was likely to be seen, he turned and muttered menacingly:

"We're not through yet, you two-legged maypole. We'll see who has the last laugh."

The one horse was a simple matter. The ranger's mare, when not wanted, was kept in the state farm stable or on the common grazing land. Selivanov got hold of her and the saddle without any trouble, according to the ranger's long-standing instructions. But he had to wheedle the other horse out of the stable lad. Now the lad was a law unto himself: depending on his mood, he might be as helpful as could be, or he might dig his heels right in. What's more, when he'd made up his mind, he'd not be swayed by any gain or gift: on the contrary, the more you tried to tempt him, the more he resisted. This time Selivanov ran up against him in just the latter kind of mood; he did, however, eventually get his way and took the second horse, without a saddle it's true, since there was none to hand.

Grabbing a couple of pitchforkfuls of hay from behind the ranger's house, he fed the horses, watered them, and, flung himself down on the stove (where he usually slept at Ivan's) without getting undressed. Sleep didn't come for ages. Selivanov was worried that Ivan might turn up that night, which would mean that he'd have to lie about the horses. He didn't want to tell the ranger the truth, not because he didn't trust him, but because he wanted to have his own secret, something to busy himself with, worry his own head about. Vague schemes and presentiments turned over in his mind. His daring had ignited and was tossing Selivanov from side to side as he lay on the stove, playing blind-man's-buff with the terror that was also sneaking about somewhere in his mind, and now and then swinging his perplexed heart back and forth like a pendulum. – Aren't I a fine figure of a man? thought Selivanov boastfully. – Yes, I really know how to take the bull by the horns. After all, luck can change from minute to minute, can't it? And if you're fated to be gored, even a polled cow can do it. You can't guard against Fate! Marriage now, that'd be even better. That'd put the finishing touch to my life." The fantasy took off: he saw himself in the *taiga* with a son, teaching him to read the spoor; clipping him over the head for being slow, slapping him on the shoulder when he was smart . . . And with this fantasy he drifted off.

He woke up punctually: they had to leave the village under cover of darkness and be in the *taiga* by dawn. He threw the saddle on quickly. He put a padded jacket and an old blanket on the second horse, and made two loops of rope which he put over its back – they'd do instead of stirrups, to make the going easier. He tossed some grub to the dogs, had some bread and cold water (which he drank through a chunk of sugarloaf), shut up the *izba* and set off through the rowan thicket, finding his way by guess and feel.

When the woman's dog gave tongue, Selivanov called him all the names he could think of. He tied the horses to the garden fence and went towards the house, where he ran into Lanky as he turned into the porch.

"Ready?"

"Get inside the *izba*!"

Svetlichnaya was fussing about in the hall. "How can you take a man away when he's so poorly? How will he get on with no one to look after him? Why can't he stay here?"

Lyudmila looked at Selivanov anxiously. She too seemed to be against all this, and when Selivanov himself looked at the sick man, doubt seeded itself in his mind also. Cheeks and brow burned, eyes shone feverishly, and though he had crumpled his handkerchief to hide it you could see it was covered in blood.

First they loaded up one horse with the smaller sacks of provisions, making sure they wouldn't get in the rider's way, then on the one without a saddle they loaded bundles of all kinds of stuff they would need in the hideout. Finally, before setting out, they each drank a stirrup-cup of vodka. Each except the officer, that is. Lyudmila, who'd clearly guessed as well as anyone what the poir t of the drink was, drank her share with the rest, trying not to cough and splutter. But her father was coughing anyway without stopping.

Bidding Svetlichnaya farewell, the officer did not risk a kiss, but he held her long by the shoulders, looked into her eyes flowing with tears, and finally spoke.

"When I made my way back to Russia, I was afraid that I wouldn't find any real people there."

"But where should they all go to?" She gave a flicker of a smile.

"Wherever God sent them. But as for you – thank you."

They settled Lyudmila in the saddle. The officer, as if momentarily forgetting his illness, jumped up on his little mare like a young blood. He cut a fine figure in the saddle, recalling

69

the dashing days of his past. But the steed beneath him had changed, everything had changed, and straightaway his face fell, darkened, and he said impatiently, "Are we going, or what?"

Selivanov took the reins from him and led the horse behind him, choosing paths through the rowan stand in the half-light of morning.

He'd have preferred mist, but the morning was clear and it promised to be sunny and hot. They had to reach the place before mid-day, and the *taiga* horses have only one pace – an unhurried walk, three *versts* an hour. You can't make them go any faster.

Selivanov wound long loops through the rowan thicket, to the brook and back (or was he following the brook's winding course?), crossing it again and again. Each time the horses went to drink, but barely managed to stretch their necks out before he pulled them on with a cry of "Gee up! Move on, now! Off to the knackers' yard?" The horses weren't in the least upset – conscious of their own competence and endurance, they would shake their manes, cast sideways looks at Selivanov's dogs frolicking round them, and go on.

In the end they emerged on to a proper path and Selivanov gave the horse's head back to the officer. The horses could follow the path themselves anyway, it was work they were used to.

They went towards Chekhardak and the very same half-finished depot where Selivanov had once acted the bandit. He had long ago dismantled the barrack building – or more accurately, adapted it and turned it into a roomy *izba* for himself. This was where he went about his affairs: boiling up antlers for medicine, tanning skins, carving up carcasses to make preserved meat; he stored traps there too, nooses, snares, even some spare guns. The path they followed was disused – that is, only Selivanov himself used it from time to time. It wound along a deep black mossy river course, and roots lay across every yard of it, like steps. To the side of the path, and even right on it, Slippery Jack mushrooms grew in nest-like clusters. Soon they began to put up all kinds of birds: here a hazel-hen, there a capercaillie or a wood pigeon. The dogs raced on far ahead, scaring everything all round, revelling in their power and liberty.

The officer started to doze on his horse. The little caravan went along in silence; only the horses snorted, and sometimes their shoes clanged when they struck an outcrop of rock on the path.

All his life, Selivanov had occupied himself only with what entered the *taiga* and what left it; and if there were no lofty thoughts in his mind in that regard, the feelings which he experienced were lofty enough: with every year that passed, he felt this natural union between himself and the *taiga* to be more meaningful. When he emerged among people, leaving the *taiga* at his back, Selivanov thought of it as an entity, whole and vital, but separate from himself, and this separation he perceived as a disruption forced on him from outside, a violation of nature and of the natural order.

But when he returned, the *taiga* again ceased to be something secondary to him, again he felt he was its brain; they were not two but one, he and the *taiga*; moreover, only in his presence did the *taiga* lay bare its face, the whole completeness of its being.

Time was he'd begrudged Ivan Ryabinin the *taiga*, but he'd quickly grasped that Ivan, all things said and done, was merely "a man in the *taiga*": he knew much, but understood little. Often, too, Selivanov was tested by a bitter vexation that his father had not lived, because it was to him in particular that he wished to show off his skill and knowledge; and yet at the same time he understood that he far outshone his father in the craft of the *taiga*, that the slights which he had had to bear from his father would be avenged if his father could glimpse with even one eye from wherever he was in this world or the next the gait with which the son trod in the father's tracks. But life is not like that, you can prove yourself only to yourself, and though there is joy in that, it is an incomplete joy.

Today, leading these strangers through the *taiga*, he experienced a mixture of feelings. He felt very differently towards each of them: the officer, his daughter, and Lanky. While he understood that none of them had anything to do with him – one was on his way to die, another to bury him, and the third – well, who could tell what dark and wicked purpose *he* might have? – while he understood this, he nonetheless wanted to amaze them with something, to show off his daring.

At the point where the path started to loop up a slope, he fell back a little as if answering a call of nature, and then belted straight up through the bushes, up the impossibly steep slope, leaping out on to the path before the others had even shown round the bend into the first loop. But when they did come round, the idiotic prank fell flat; he even began to feel ashamed, since far from being amazed, they failed even to notice what he'd done, so burdened were they all with their own thoughts.

And Selivanov was suddenly overcome with a terrible melancholy, a melancholy on account of everything: his whole life: that part of his life that had already passed and was preserved in his memory; the part passing right now, without visible connection with the future, whatever lay ahead.

Selivanov feared this melancholy. He, a man of the *taiga*, who all too often had to look underfoot and rarely managed to glance at the heavens, was indifferent to questions of faith (there was just never time to think about it), yet he considered his state of melancholy a sin, in the most literal sense. Melancholy was to him the enemy of life, he felt it was the one thing that could break him – that is, if he descended into melancholy, like drink. Melancholy – the voice from nowhere; melancholy, which is emptiness, resides in every person like a seed waiting to sprout. God forbid it should. When melancholy revealed itself at its most naked, it was death. Selivanov had seen it more than once in the eyes of a dying animal, when it had already lost the breath of life; then, in that short instant, melancholy ripped the soul out of the body and took it away into nowhere, and its last dark business was the last living flicker in eyes already dead. Selivanov always tried not to look into such eyes, because of the feeling they evoked in him that the alien melancholy might turn out to be dangerously catching. In it everything lost its bonds, and meaning flew away; the tree was left to itself, the sky to itself; and the beast under sky and tree, unconnected with the soul of either the one or the other; and man looks around and everything is against him, and he against everything; and then you begin to think that everything in the world, from the smallest blade of grass up to the sun, exists in an order quite different from what you'd thought before, and that this order is detached from you on all sides, and the thought makes you want to howl . . .

When Selivanov was taken this way, he surrendered to malice to save himself; it was the only way out with melancholy, that loathsome reptile. Drunkenness (he tried to drown himself in liquor) made him go all soft and flabby, like a huge fat backside, and it was hard to salvage himself from fits of drunken slobbering. But if you vented your malice on someone, now – that allowed you to feel ashamed, tick yourself off, say you were sorry – and then you were a person again! Sometimes you just had to let go – kick the dog in the guts, say, so it would let out a yelp of doggy pain and give you a look of saintly reproach, and you would feel ashamed; and then pity would wash all the blackness out of your soul. Or you might take an axe to a pine too young to have resin yet. You'd see it twitching and trembling, then drops would appear where your axe had struck . . . Then you'd scrape resin with your knife off an older pine and smear it on the wound, and, for all the wanton stupidity of what you'd done, the tree would heal itself.

Sometimes Selivanov took his malice out on a person. That meant curing himself by fear: it was usually a strong man he picked a quarrel with in his melancholy; and as soon as the terror of a beating got through to his consciousness, his soul was cleansed and was again in touch with normality.

After the climb, they walked for a long time on level ground, then made a halt by a brook. It so happened that the other men went off into the bushes together, leaving Selivanov and Lyudmila in private. Unexpectedly she asked him, "You're a man who knows the way of the world, can you tell me how much longer he has to live?"

Selivanov snapped his eyes shut, remembering the officer's warning. He tried to look daft. She frowned in irritation.

"Look, please don't pretend you don't know anything! I trust you, don't try to deceive me."

She sounded so sad that Selivanov himself was saddened.

"How did you find that out, eh? He told me to keep mum."

"Him," she gestured after Lanky. "But I'd have guessed on my own, anyway."

"And why should he've gone and told you that?"

"Oh heavens!" She rested her head on the trunk of the pine tree whose roots they were sitting on – Selivanov didn't dare warn her that resin was sure to drop on her hair. "Heavens above! Why should it matter who said what? How long has he left to live?"

How on earth could Selivanov know that?

"I've a cure for him – a root; we'll treat him, maybe he'll pull through."

He raised no hope in her eyes. No, they were still full of subdued sorrow.

"And why's *he* come along? What's in it for him?" Selivanov asked probingly.

"He's Papa's evil genius . . ."

"He's what?"

"He's fighting for an idea. But then again, I don't know. Maybe he really is fighting, but he's evil all the same. Look, don't rub him up the wrong way, will you." Here she seemed to shrink into herself, and looked around quickly. "I'm afraid of him!"

"Don't be afraid!" Selivanov trembled with joy. "I've seen plenty worse than him!"

She looked at him sceptically, and Selivanov could see why. Well, after all, he wasn't too scary looking, was he? Ivan, now – he was a different matter! But at the moment there was still no knowing which of them would turn out worthy of the lass.

"Don't be afraid!" He gave her a wink. And at that moment he feared nothing himself either.

So what happened next? They settled down in the cabin. Father and daughter on the bunk, Selivanov and Lanky in the loft. Selivanov chased round after roots, brewed up a potion and dosed the sick man, who drank it down, wrinkling his face and gagging. Lanky loafed about the forest for days at a time, shooting at woodpeckers with his pistol, and fell into bed early in the evenings. But Selivanov often sat up until late on his block of wood in the corner, listening to the conversations between father and daughter and putting in a word now and again himself if it was opportune.

After a week (he couldn't drag it out any longer), he led the horses back to the village. The stable-man abused him roundly and shook his fists at him. Ivan grabbed Selivanov by the front of his coat when he saw him, all but lifting him off the ground.

"What were you doing with the horses?"

Selivanov produced a whole stream of plausible fibs, plucked his shirt back to show his chest and swore blind (cross his heart and hope to die) that he'd done nothing wrong, far from it, and that never again in all his born days would he so much as go near Ivan's mare, because she guzzled so much, and then the sounds that came out of her and the smell – the game couldn't get away fast enough wherever she went.

Ivan didn't believe a word of it, but he could only hold out so long against Selivanov's nonsense; he growled to himself, eyes flashing, and then cooled down.

The following morning Selivanov returned to Chekhardak. He was more than a hundred paces from the cabin when he met the officer on the path and took fright.

"It's all right, I'm only out for a walk!" the officer reassured him.

"Where . . . are the others?"

"Asleep, would you believe! And what a marvellous morning! Aren't you tired? Look at your knapsack!"

Selivanov had certainly packed the stuff in – bread, flour, fat bacon, vegetables. Svetlichnaya had gone to a lot of trouble.

"Why not sit down? Have a rest, do!" suggested the officer, and Selivanov realised that he wanted to talk. He slipped the straps and leaned the knapsack against a stump; then he chose the driest spot he could, and they sat down. Before their eyes was the summit of the hill from which Selivanov had once so deftly sniped at the commanders with stars on their shoulders. He terribly wanted to boast about it (there'd never be another chance), so that his skill would be admired as it should. He held his tongue, though – now wasn't the time to talk about it. All this while, the other man was silent. The sun seemed to have despaired of breathing its life-giving force into him; it was reflected stark off the pallor of his face, or glanced off him. And in that face itself elusive changes were taking place.

"Do you believe in God?" asked the officer.

Selivanov hadn't expected a question like that; he waited awhile, thinking what best to say.

"It's a sin not to believe, but belief's a fair queer thing," he mumbled, afraid that the other would see through his slyness, but he seemed not even to hear the reply. He looked at the top of Selivanov's hill, or somewhere beyond, and rocked a little.

"So many strong and healthy people have tried to get into Russia and perished! But *I* got through . . . And if God is behind this, how can we tell what he wills us to do, and what would be our ruin?"

He fell silent. Selivanov tried to expand on the subject.

"When the sun's in your eyes, thinking about God's more than you can manage, but at night – that's another matter."

"You're right," the officer agreed with him earnestly. "The sun makes the world look flat, but at night you get a new perspective, you can get right to the essence of things. Light coming through the dark . . . light in the darkness . . . But it's already too late for me to get to the bottom of that, even though that's how life started. And there was *Verity*, and that seemed to be enough – but then it seemed to become covered with a haze, it became no more than habit. And life carried on of its own accord . . ."

Selivanov felt like a dog listening, ears pricked up, in the hope of catching a familiar word in human speech. But he wasn't a dog, he was a man; and for that reason he thought to himself that behind all the different kinds of wisdom, something very simple lay concealed, and that he'd known clearly all along what it was; if other people made things out to be complicated, then it was either because they couldn't speak simply, or because they wanted to look very clever.

"Do you think my daughter's beautiful?" the officer asked without warning.

Selivanov expressed his admiration for her.

"But have you noticed how she says the word 'papa'? It's as though she's learning how to say it, listening to herself say it. I'm like that too . . . she and I are learning how to be father and daughter. I'm sure you've noticed how she sometimes pronounces the word 'papa' just to hear the sound of it. You see, if she said it at all earlier, it was only in her thoughts, or in a whisper. But one must feel quite different, mustn't one, when someone actually answers to the word. It's only then that it sounds as it should."

There were steps behind them.

"Heavens above, Papa, I didn't know what to think! Why on earth did you go out alone?"

There were tears in her eyes. She hadn't had time to brush her hair since waking, she was barefoot and in her petticoat.

77

She sank down on her knees by her father and touched his hands with a careful, shy caress. What was couched in that touch was so precious that Selivanov turned his eyes away, vexed with himself and quivering with envy. Is it possible, is he really going to die? For the first time he thought seriously about it, and discovered an unfamiliar sensation of creeping terror somewhere below his heart, almost in his stomach. Though he had both seen death and brought it on others himself, it seemed he hadn't ever come to grips with the real terror of death, because he'd never known pity.

"I'll be going then . . ." he mumbled, confused, and shouldered his knapsack.

"You too!" the officer told his daughter. "I'll sit out here a while. Go on! Go on! Help Andrian Nikanorych unpack the groceries, fill the kettle, he's been a long way . . ."

Reluctantly, but dutifully, she got up, and, without saying a word, walked up the path in front of Selivanov. After a few steps, he noticed that her shoulders were shaking with silent tears.

"Don't break your heart, you'll only make the pain worse for him!" Selivanov whispered behind her. "You must keep him from thinking dark thoughts. They'll only push him further down the road. Understand?"

She nodded.

"Not thinking about his illness and taking the root medicine, that's his only hope!"

"When Mama was alive, she always talked about him as though he weren't living. I was used to his simply not being there. And suddenly, there he was! He truly has risen from the dead for a little while, and now he's leaving again . . . I can't bear it!"

She sank down on to the moss and cried out loud.

The knapsack stopped Selivanov from sitting down next to her, but he stooped as far as his load allowed and whispered earnestly, "Stop, I say! Hey now, listen! Stop right now, this instant! You've got to understand, God sent him from that world so he could know what it is to have a daughter! Just think how many kids were left orphans forever after that carnage!"

She didn't take in his words, because she saw no justice in them, only truth, a truth which she knew, and knew well. Better, perhaps, that she had not known it!

"How can I go on living!" she cried. And Selivanov was at a loss to know how to answer, but he took her firmly by the shoulders and pulled her to her feet.

"They'll hear you!" he then said.

This did work: she hurried off down the path, looking round anxiously and shuddering as she wept.

Lanky, all puffy with sleep, met them by the cabin. He looked at them suspicously.

"Where's Nikolai Aleksandrovich?"

"Out walking," Selivanov answered offhandedly, barging past him with his knapsack through the cabin door.

And what happened then? Well, there was that summer night when Nikolai Aleksandrovich told his daughter and Selivanov about himself. The moonlight had time to wander from one window to the one on the opposite side, the lamp-wick was trimmed three times, and three times the kettle came to the boil. That night the sick man's cough left him in peace, and you could imagine he might be going to recover.

He talked about how he'd lived in poverty in China after crossing the border; about how Colonel Bakmetev had died in strange circumstances; about how he'd gone to Europe and set up there as a chauffeur; about how the company of the White Army exiles, living true to their flag, had given him a new rush of hope; about how he'd found a woman . . . He talked about this too, although he didn't say how it was that he'd lost her.

Selivanov felt that this conversation was in the nature of a confession. But not entirely. Although there is not a man who has ever lived who is unspotted and without sin, the sick man

79

kept quiet about that side of his life; instead, he talked about his life as he would have liked to have seen it, as the vision which he wanted to convey to his daughter. Selivanov found his story interesting, if hard to understand. He wanted to hear what the "White" truth was; the officer's story, though, was all of nobility, as if the truth were self-evident. And for Selivanov that truth, the "White" truth, which appeared only in flashes in the story, was preferable to the "Red" truth for one reason only; because it didn't affect him personally in any way, it didn't loom menacingly in his life, it flew past with its proud words somewhere far above his head, leaving Selivanov with the right to believe in his "third" truth. He felt the same unkind pity for those men who'd fallen in the name of the "Red" truth as he did for those who'd fallen in the name of the "White" truth; he remembered with gratitude how his father had saved him from passions alien to him; and he felt a sense of pride in the fact that he hadn't stuck his nose into other people's business. He wondered who, if every Russian peasant man had had views like his, would have been left to do the fighting. The Reds and the Whites had made use of the peasants so they could smash each other to pieces, but if the peasants had stayed true to their own truth, what would've happened then?

Seizing his chance, he asked cautiously, "Now, say, if the peasant men hadn't gone over either to the Whites or the Reds, how would it have turned out then?"

The officer looked surprised, then his look darkened; he didn't answer at once.

"That's a meaningless question! You call them 'peasants', but they're part of the people as a whole, they can't go their own way . . ."

Selivanov interrupted quickly.

"Look at me. I went my own way, my dad did too . . ."

The officer flapped his hands in irritation.

"Chance. This is the backwoods. So you didn't help the Whites: that means you helped the Reds. Sitting on the fence is a kind of help too."

Selivanov wanted to say something, but Lyudmila got there first.

"But, Papa, that's what *they* say: 'Whoever is not with us is against us'!"

"And they're right. Whoever is not with them, is against them."

She shook her head sceptically.

"Because I was a White officer's daughter – Mama and I didn't try to hide it – they wouldn't take me at the institute. I could only get work through connections . . . But am I really against them?"

She spoke as if asking herself that question. Selivanov jumped in eagerly, "That's egsakly what I'm saying! It's *them* who are against! We all go our own way!"

Paying no heed to what Selivanov had said, father answered daughter:

"What are you, then, a Young Communist? Yes? So you believe in their kennel communism? No! You don't really, do you?"

"Of course I don't! They're evil! They don't even believe each other! But . . ."

"That says it all! You don't have to say any more! The main thing is that no one should believe in *them*! Although . . ."

At that instant the moon appeared, framed in yet another window pane, and a yellow light fell on his face, which was shielded from the lamplight by a pillow.

"Although one cannot live long in unbelief. No, that is quite impossible! And because people want to live, they'll believe anything, however absurd. I've travelled all over Russia . . . It's terrible, there's no way out."

"All the same, I've gone my own way!" Selivanov stood his ground obstinately.

"If you had, you wouldn't have helped me."

Selivanov jabbed a finger at where Lanky was sleeping.

"I wouldn't help him. I'm helping a *good* man."

"There are no good men!" the officer hit back sharply.

"There are only those who are right and those who are wrong."

"And what's he?" Selivanov jabbed his finger at Lanky again.

The officer was obviously embarrassed.

"Struggle makes men bitter . . . Idealists are the first to die."

This was no answer and Selivanov grunted to himself smugly. But the whole conversation was useful to him: it confirmed *his own* faith in the truth.

He was accustomed to classifying everything in life, not just individual people, in the terms and according to the forms of the *taiga*, because that way things were clear to him, it was a way of translating life's many voices into a language he could understand and grasp. The power that held sway "there", everywhere beyond the edge of the *taiga*, he imagined as a furious wild boar, rooted to the ground not only by its four hog trotters, but by every ounce of its clumsy flesh. A dangerous animal without a doubt! But what were skill and wit for, if not to get the better of him?

The "White" truth on the other hand, as painted by the officer, Selivanov saw as a wild forest goat with powerful horns on his head, hanging in the air with a graceful, distant leap, or with head lowered in readiness to fight off any opponent with a flourish of his horns. But when he leaps high, the goat can be hit by a bullet all the more easily, and his horns are over-twisty to be good weapons. So the boar had done the goat in!

But what sort of animal did you need to be to survive under the boar's rule? Easy – a wolverine! A nasty little beast, mean enough for two. But Selivanov knew better than to fancy he was a beast like that . . .

The full moon, a perfect disc, showed in the window of the cabin, and everything took on new shapes under its relentless light. It seemed they were all afraid to recognise it as an evil portent – which is what it was . . .

From that night on, during the next day and the next, everything began to draw swiftly and steadily towards the close. Selivanov rushed to the village once again for supplies; Svetlichnaya howled as she packed his bag. The dogs at the depot were anxious and unhappy; Selivanov had to put them on a leash to keep them from being underfoot.

Lyudmila looked at her father dwindling away and dwindled herself, looking pinched and wan; her eyes glittered drily. Lanky grew more sullen every day. Though the days were sunny and still, the nights warm, the sick man felt cold day and night. His chill transmitted itself to everyone, and Selivanov often caught the girl looking at him, as if she, and everyone else there, was soon to die. Worse still, Selivanov picked up a cough himself; he would cover his mouth with his hand, then carefully study his palm to see if there was blood, though he never really believed he could be ill.

There were no more long conversations in the evening, but the officer managed to utter the phrase which Selivanov had been waiting for: "Don't leave my daughter!" He said this to him when they were one to one, and though Selivanov merely nodded his head once, it enabled the man to die in peace – as far, that is, as anyone can die peacefully.

When the end came, in the middle of the night, the dogs howled not at all, contrary to popular belief. Lyudmila turned to stone where she stood by the plank bunk; Lanky was stooped at the door. Selivanov still couldn't believe it. He raced about, unable to discern any obvious difference between the dead and the living. Seeing no sign of life in the others, he threw up his hands, and seemed not to have the strength to think what words he should say in such circumstances. There was something entirely unfamiliar at work in his mind, something that had been completely absent when his father had died. If someone had told him that this was pity, he would have been indignant. But his heart was overcome with lassitude, he felt so poorly, almost nauseated, and there was nothing left for him but to wonder at himself.

At dawn he began to make the coffin from an old stock of boards. He tried to make as little noise as possible, looking round toward the cabin fearfully with almost every blow of the hammer, as if someone might appear and shame him.

The most awful thing was that it had fallen silent all about; silence had come, though only a single voice – not even that, a cough – had vanished from the *taiga*. And this was yet another upset of all Selivanov's previous notions, chiefly those relating to himself. What were these people to him, who had turned up on his path by chance? He had existed before them and would exist after them! Wasn't that how it was?

But the *taiga* was mute . . .

In the late afternoon they buried him. A lifeless pallor had appeared on Lyudmila's face. She did everything in silence, not looking at anyone, and, it seemed, not seeing anyone. Selivanov neatly covered the grave with green turf, then Lanky stood by it and uttered a speech no one wanted to hear, except himself. He spoke of honour and of the struggle. They fired a volley with the pistol and gun, then there was nothing more to do. Lyudmila said that she wanted to be alone for a while. Selivanov thought of hiding himself in the bushes, just in case; who knew what might enter the lass's head in her despair? But Lanky took him into the cabin for a talk.

"You're going to work with me."

"Work, how d'ye mean?" Selivanov didn't understand.

"None of your play-acting now, and just you forget your little jokes!" Lanky replied menacingly. "If I send someone along, you do as he tells you!"

"What someone?" Selivanov asked again, wracked by a fit of shivering.

"Don't play the fool with me!" replied Lanky, still more nastily. "I'll get at you from the other side of the grave if I have to."

Selivanov realised it was best to agree. But he wasn't a man who could be bound, like some lackey! The lad was a greenhorn all right! If he'd been smarter, he'd have asked Selivanov for help or advice; and Selivanov might not have refused. He covered his eyes so as not to give away his thoughts, and pretended to be afraid, feigning servility as best he could.

"Her," Lanky motioned in the direction of the grave, "I'll find a new place for her. We'll stay in touch through her. She'll be your niece."

Selivanov tensed as he would before a critical shot. – The fool! He wanted to mix the lass up in it too! He'd make a mess of it right away and drag her down with him! –

Only a minute before Selivanov had felt that he was the officer's successor. It was to him, him specifically, that the father had entrusted his daughter as if giving her in adoption. But now this long streak of piss wanted to take her away on account of his fool fancies . . . No, never! –

He decided to try the nice way first.

"Listen, say I do whatever you want, but the lass, now . . . well, that's up to her! Let her live her own life!"

The man looked contemptuously at him.

"Live? Her life is vengeance for her father, the continuation of his work. There's no other life for her!"

"Asked her, have you?"

"Shut your mouth!" Lanky snapped at him.

Should I snuff him out, then? He'll finish her! – But he realised he couldn't. There was something tying him to Lanky, it felt like a trap snapped round his foot. Think! You've got to think! Don't let the lass go! –

"I'm leaving today. To find somewhere for her. Wait for me here. And watch it!"

"What else? Of course! We'll be here!" Selivanov babbled happily. – A breathing space! What a fool! What a right bloody fool! Not the first idea of how people work!

Later, when they talked about this among the three of them, Lyudmila listened with indifference. Perhaps she didn't understand what they were talking about, or perhaps she really didn't care about her ultimate fate. Selivanov tried to convey

85

by transparent hints what Lanky wanted, but he had no success. She agreed to everything. Lanky interpreted her silence as a suitable response. He took the role of head, and perhaps he was, at that – though not as far as Selivanov was concerned.

Lanky left that evening. But the conversation which Selivanov had been banking on having after he'd been left alone with Lyudmila didn't work out as he'd hoped. It was as though she was in a dream: she heard nothing, understood nothing, sat motionless on the bunk and refused food. In the end, Selivanov forced her to eat something and lie down. He couldn't bring himself to lie down in the dead man's place and sat on his block of wood by the table, putting his head in the crook of his elbow; but as always when he had something important and risky to do the next morning, he couldn't get off to sleep.

In the morning he announced without any explanation: "We're going today! Better get ready!"

At first she didn't take this in at all. Then she cast her eyes at the bunk, neatly covered with a blanket, where her father had lain only the day before, gave a start and ran out of the cabin. She was already by the grave when Selivanov caught up with her. She fell on the grave, and at last let her tears well up, for the first time; Selivanov breathed a sigh of relief. He retreated through the trees, sat down on some moss and prepared to wait.

An hour passed and she lay exhausted, face grubby with tears and earth. Selivanov resolutely picked her up and took her into the cabin. He made her wash, get ready and eat before taking to the road.

The dogs raised hell. To be left without their master, but with other people, that they could just about accept. But when they were told that their master was leaving and they would be left alone, they jumped up on their hind legs and choked at their collars, howling dolefully and shrilly to the whole *taiga*.

86

Selivanov shut them up, making as if to thrash them. "Sit, you bastards! I'm coming back today! I told you, I'm coming back today!"

The howling turned to whimpering, the sound following them along the path until they rounded the first bend.

Selivanov soon turned off the main path, however. After half a mile or so's scrambling over stones and obstacles, he led Lyudmila on to a small path – more of a game trail than a path for people – that was nearly invisible in the long grass and gave out entirely in stony patches. He wanted to take no chances that Lanky might suddenly take it into his head to return. After the third *verst* Lyudmila was out of breath; they stopped three or four more times after that. Selivanov didn't hurry. It was almost evening when they emerged at Ryabinovka, but they spent a while stealing through the thickets, so as to approach the ranger's house from the blind side where no one would see them.

He left the girl in the bushes and squinting about him and bent low, he brushed quickly past the gate. Then he frowned in irritation: Ivan was home.

"So you're back, you old vagrant?" the master of the house greeted him.

Selivanov, without even a greeting, without any warning, blurted out: "There's a problem, Vanya!"

He was worried at leaving Lyudmila alone.

"Been up to something, eh?" the ranger looked at him suspiciously.

"A person's in trouble, Vanya. A fine person. We must help!"

Ryabinin looked at him even more suspiciously.

"Can I fetch the person? Then I'll explain everything. We must help! I'll do it right now!"

It had suddenly come into his head that Lyudmila might not stay where she was, she might wander off somewhere . . . He flew past the gate, threw himself into the bushes, found her and breathed easy again.

"Well, everything's all right then! Let's go!"

Ryabinin stood guardedly in the middle of the entrance. Pleased, Selivanov saw the ranger's eyes widen, saw how his hands flew to his shirt, which was hanging out of his trousers, how he choked on his tongue, trying to find a reply to Lyudmila's soft greeting. He bustled about the house in distraction, helpless, speechless, then implored Selivanov with a look, "What do I do with her? Tell me!"

"What're ye rushing about there for, Vanya, now?" Selivanov said patronisingly, all fatherly reproach. "A person needs feeding: fifteen *versts* we've done today!"

Although Lyudmila wasn't feeling herself and was tired from the journey she suddenly began to feel sorry for this tall, rangy, man who was standing all hunched in his embarrassment. When yet another plate crashed from his hands, she stood up and offered to help. He silently yielded his place at the cooker and looked disconsolately at Selivanov. At that instant, when they were together for a second, she a silver thread, he a hank of coarse yarn, Selivanov had a sudden thought: that, say, it would make an interesting pattern, the coarse cloth with a silver thread running through it . . . Actually it wasn't a thought, more a whim really . . . Lanky would look way better next to her.

He remembered Lanky and his stomach turned over – Maybe better let it all go to hell, get out to Bald Hill, or even further than that. Let Lanky and the ranger lock horns together! But he knew that Ivan would never be able to brazen it out against that one; he'd step aside – he didn't have the right to stay put, come to that. The knowledge that he alone, Andrian Nikanorych Selivanov, could undo this tricky knot filled him with such pride in himself that he even started shouting at the ranger: "Stop showing off. It's not called for! If you can't be master in your own house, get out the way, and we . . ."

Ivan looked at him reproachfully, and stood in the middle of the hut like a great drooping larch. Selivanov winked at him and they went out. On the porch step Ivan gave the other man a dog-like look. Selivanov felt very much like boasting, but there wasn't time – he still had the return journey to Chekhardak in front of him that day.

"Well, you see now, she's an orphan. I buried her father at Chekhardak yesterday. There's nowhere to put her up. You know very well what kind of a home I've got. So then, Vanya, will you have her to stay a while, then we can think of something?"

Of course, this was hardly enough said to make things clear, and Ivan tried to argue. He asked, how come they'd ended up in Chekhardak, and so on, but Selivanov hadn't the time to explain, anyway he couldn't be bothered. Besides, she'd best tell him herself, so she could choose what he ought to know, and what not.

"Well, Van', I've got to get back to Chekhardak tonight. There's one little job there I've still got to do. Make sure you don't offend the lass, now!"

Ryabinin looked at him as though he'd gone barmy, got up and went into the house.

"Don't shut the door, please!" Lyudmila asked, standing flush-faced by the cooker. Ivan opened all the windows, but outside the heat hadn't yet abated and the house got no cooler, though a pleasant draught came in. Ivan went off to change his shirt and brush his hair while Selivanov wasn't looking. He hadn't had time to shave; now and again he rubbed his chin in irritation. He was already himself once more, although he was still avoiding Lyudmila's eye.

So what? thought Selivanov. Only twelve years older than she is! If she hadn't been a fine lady, and he a rough country man, they'd have been a fine match! – But the more he thought about it, the funnier it was. Eeeh, look at the way she moves her hands, see her standing on tiptoe. She has a look could fair freeze off an ordinary man. But it could cause Ivan a lot of heartache, that look of hers. –

Selivanov thought of his father's sister, the one who was married to a skilled craftsman and lived in Irkutsk. He hadn't had news of her in a hundred years, but he remembered where she was living. He made up his mind to settle Lyudmila with her the first chance he had, and then see. The more he looked at the ranger, the more he was convinced he should get him out of trouble as quick as he could.

Despite Lyudmila's protests, Ivan didn't sit at the table. – Quite proper, too! – thought Selivanov. – Or he'd be making slurping noises with his spoon in no time! – Selivanov himself was slurping out of his spoon for all he was worth. What of it! He was only a peasant and always would be! That lass, though, look at her sipping her soup from the edge of her spoon instead of sticking the spoon right full into her trap! If he's going to suck at it like that, it'll take him till morning to fill up! Aagh, now he's taking little bits of bread with his spoon, and he's already dirtied the tablecloth, and his trousers! –

Selivanov wiped the sleeve of his shirt across his mouth, then across his trousers, belched and stood up.

"But that was good! Really shouldn't have! Can hardly walk!"

"Perhaps you don't need to go . . . not today?" Lyudmila asked shyly and looked him in the eye with an anxiety that only they two understood. Selivanov didn't let on about his own worry. He replied as if he hadn't understood that look:

"I've got my dogs out there! You mustn't leave them long on a leash in the *taiga*, they might go wild."

Ivan drew him to one side and asked him in a whisper, "If she's here, then where do I go? Or what?"

"Where do you go?" asked Selivanov, exasperated. "What, and leave her in the house alone? What's got into you, Vanya?"

Ivan stumbled over his words. "It's not the done thing . . . Alone in the house, with an ordinary bloke . . ."

"That's just it, with an ordinary bloke. Nothing wrong with that. An officer, now, that'd be different!"

Ivan understood and felt hurt, though he gave no sign of it. Selivanov felt hurt too. Although the ranger was his junior by far, still, it would never have occurred to Selivanov that a young lass, and what's more, a young lady even, might be made to feel uncomfortable by his presence. This great bear, though, thought she might take *him* for something different.

When he was saying goodbye to Lyudmila, he whispered, "You explain to him about all that . . . you know, whatever you want."

"When are you coming back?"

He spread his hands.

"Please don't quarrel out there . . . It means nothing to me, wherever I go . . . Perhaps he's right, I should go with him . . ."

It was this indifference of hers that Selivanov feared most.

"You have to live!"

"What for?"

"So you can have babies!" he said spitefully. Lyudmila wasn't embarrassed and didn't take exception; all she did was to give his hands the lightest touch. "I'm so grateful to you for everything! Please try to be good!"

Night overtook Selivanov about three *versts* from the cabin. Though he wasn't given to mysticism, the *taiga* at night was a mysterious phenomenon to him. He believed, or more accurately he imagined, that at night everything living and not living is liberated from reality, the essence of which is compulsion and necessity. Trees, rocks, grass, animals, even people, while they are alive are always in need of something and are needed in some way themselves. If there were no night, would man really find the strength to walk, the trees to stand, the stones to lie on the ground? But night approaches, and, becoming unseen, everything living and not living dissolves into a peaceful mirage amidst the darkness, where there is no tension of distinctions and rivalry. This state of affairs is a mystery for the eyes. And so, if a person walks along a path at night and his eyes distinguish something, trees, stones, and the path itself are forced to assume their daytime mask, so as not to bring the wakeful intruder into collision with those at rest.

When he had to travel by night, Selivanov felt both envy and malicious triumph. He envied everything that resided in the gloom at either side, everything at liberty from its own confines. But then everything that was accessible to his eye was forced to reassume its own face; and Selivanov would whisper venomously into the dark: "Well, come on! Come on! Gone soft, have you, or why don't you show?" And in front of him, out of the dim outlines, almost unwilling, a stump or a stone grew unhurriedly. Passing by them, Selivanov would say jubilantly, "You see!" But he had hardly walked five steps before it was obvious that the stump or stone had slipped away again into darkness and peace. There was something else he knew, too: never strike a match when you're going along a path at night. You might not give the things which are sleeping, in their dissolved state, time to recover themselves, and they might mistake their proper forms when still half-awake – so a pine bough might turn into a paw with claws, a stump into a bear, and the path itself roll up into a ball.

Another thing: when you're sitting by a bonfire at night, try throwing on some dry pine branches! When the fire bursts into flame, you'll see monsters start to dance all round; how the *taiga* moans, how all the things that have left themselves cry out, caught unawares in unseemly formlessness!

And there are other times too! When the new moon, a thin spare sickle, hangs over the wooded rise, not intruding on the eye, not dimming the stars; while in another half of the sky the stars are so bright that it seems man and the stars are the only things in their original forms amidst the darkness and shadow. It's not that the stars are any closer; it's that the sky itself is also the place where man resides, as well as on the earth and with everything that is in it and around it. Man may be like a small insect, but he is also the son of heaven.

*

Son of earth and heaven, Selivanov went along the night path towards the cabin in the section of *taiga* called Chekhardak – which gets its name from the view from the main rise down on to the knolls below, which look like drunkards leaping over one another in an insane game of leapfrog, *chekharda*.

Selivanov moved along, listening to the night, and soon he heard what he was waiting for – at the depot the tethered dogs were howling as if possessed by demons, howling as if over a corpse. In fact they were howling from fear of the night and because of their hurt feelings at what their master had done. And when he querulously untied them, they fell into such a fit of ecstatic whimpering that he took his boot to them. Their ecstasy, however, was not diminished, nor was it increased when their master fed them, for dogs do not live by bread alone.

He boiled a kettle for himself and drank his tea without anything added. Then he sat a while by the small stove and lay on the bunk without undressing, propping his gun by the wall, ready to hand . . .

Selivanov was knackered. He should have got up as early as possible, but when he heard the dogs barking he decided not to jump up from the bunk after all; his sleepy face might make him look as if he was scared, and it was so dark in the cabin that he could conceal it, as well as any real fear he might feel. There was time for the thought to pass through his head that Lanky was certainly no slouch to have got back here in only a day. He'd gone all out, but even so he was too late!

Bursting through the doorway hands, feet and head first, Lanky barked in a would-be playful tone: "Time to get up!"

Selivanov unhurriedly lifted his head and raised himself slightly, then got himself into a sitting position and rubbed his eyes ostentatiously. Lanky strode over from the threshold right to Lyudmila's bunk, had a good look, then asked, "Where is she?"

"What do you mean, where?" Selivanov gave an amazed gasp. "She left with you!"

"What?" His voice was hoarse.

"Yes, right after you left, she said she was going with you, and ran out after you. Didn't she catch up with you?" Selivanov's voice shook with sincere puzzlement.

"This is all I needed!" Lanky sat himself down on the bunk. "And what did you do? Why didn't you stop her?"

"How on earth could I? I did tell her! She didn't stay to listen!"

"You should have gone with her, you fool!"

"But you said yourself I should wait here!"

Selivanov's heart leapt at this point; he knew he was the victor and didn't bother to hide it in his voice. Lanky got up and approached Selivanov, grabbed his shirt in his fist, nearly choking him, and hauled him up.

"You're lying!"

"What are you on about?" Selivanov croaked.

Lanky wanted to look into his eyes, but it was gloomy in the cabin. With a jerk he pulled Selivanov off the bunk and dragged him towards the door. Selivanov yelped without letting up, and tried to grope for his gun with one hand, but couldn't reach it. With a kick up the backside Lanky propelled him over the threshold, still without letting go of his shirt, shook him, and set him on his feet. He looked Selivanov fiercely in the eye.

"You're lying, you vermin! It's written all over your horrible mug! You're lying! Are you trying to pull a fast one?" He was still hoping Lyudmila was somewhere there.

"Like I told you, she ran out after you!" Selivanov whined, by now sounding completely insincere; he heard the falseness in his own voice and shivered with terror, but did not weaken. A blow meant to break his jaw landed instead on his skull. Almost losing consciousness, Selivanov flopped on to the ground. Fear and terror, more than pain, preserved his self-possession. Half-blinded by the blood which had gushed into his eyes, he jumped to his feet and took off, yelping like a puppy. Behind him, a shot snapped out like the lash of a horsewhip. Selivanov fell, hardly knowing whether he was dead or alive.

"Get up!" The shout assailed his ears.

He lifted himself on to all fours. The tiny black pupil of a revolver was staring him in the eye.

"Here, vermin!"

Selivanov crawled a little way, shaking the blood from his brow, then got up, and seeming to grope at the air in front of him, approached Lanky with faltering step. He whispered something in an unsteady voice. Near to, the muzzle of the revolver looked just as teeny; but in that teeniness sat half-a-dozen deaths which would do not just for the weak, but for the best of men, the skilled and the bold. That dark little hole in the chunk of iron was stronger than them all.

"Now tell me everything," Lanky said savagely, speaking through his teeth.

"I'll tell you! I'll tell you . . . !" Selivanov babbled, nodding his head quickly. Suddenly he realised that he might really tell everything, lead Lanky straight there, and then he would lose . . . He couldn't remember what it was he had found of such value that he couldn't afford to lose it, but he knew it was about as valuable as life itself.

"I'll tell, I'll tell . . ." he babbled again. Lanky stuck his pistol in his pocket and stepped forwards. And then something – not fear of a beating, nor even fear of death, but the inability to choose the lesser of these two fears, and the despair caused by his own powerlessness – made Selivanov hurl himself at Lanky's arm. Taken by surprise, the other man jerked aside – and Selivanov flew beyond his grasp and in through the open door of the cabin. "Aaargh, you swine!" Lanky growled, flinging himself after Selivanov. But right at the threshold he was struck as though by a battering ram of monstrous power. Chest ripped open, he stumbled on to the grass.

When not only life, but blood too had long drained from the body, Selivanov was still standing at the threshold, holding his gun at the ready. Lanky seemed even lankier now. He lay as though he might jump up at any moment. Selivanov couldn't make up his mind to cross the threshold. Wracked by shivers, he couldn't even tear his hand from the gun to brush away the blood that had poured into his right eye, or wipe his lips.

The dogs had come haring along at the sound of the shots. They didn't come close, but paced about worriedly a few yards away from Lanky, drawing in the taint of blood that seemed to fill the whole *taiga*.

"Oh my, oh my!" Selivanov groaned. He raised the gun and put one foot across the threshold. "Lord above!"

Approaching the body, he poked Lanky's foot with the barrel, then, gun at the ready, walked all round him. He couldn't take in what had happened. He felt that he had never wanted this, had never intended it. Squatting in front of the dead man, he laid his gun on his knees and shook his head. The terror passed and turned to apathy. Selivanov wanted to sit down or lie on the grass, but Lanky's blood seemed to have seeped into the ground wherever he looked.

It was true what Ivan said. I am a killer – he thought.

Finally he laid the gun to one side and crawled towards Lanky and, having touched his shoulder timidly, turned him on his back.

"I had to!" he cried out. Lanky's face was exactly as it had been a half hour before, when he was still alive.

What is it that happens to a person? thought Selivanov. Everything stays exactly the way it was – face, hands, feet, but it's already not a person, it's a spent cartridge case. A lifeless person isn't a person if there's no life in him! Then what are you left with? Is a man life, then? Any life? What *is* life, if it can be there and then not be there? Start and end? Where does it go to when it ends? One pop, and then no life? And after a day, there's only rot left. Where does it all go to? –

He was on the point of lifting his eyes to the sky, but it annoyed him, it was so blue and bright, and what's more it was going its own way, remote from him.

Maybe life goes off into the earth and builds up there drop by drop? Maybe earthquakes happen because a lot of it's built up there, a pool of departed human spirit?

Suddenly Selivanov winced as his throbbing cut forehead began to itch, and he remembered his injury, the blood all over his face.

"You just lie there a while," he said to Lanky. "We'll think of something later."

Right then, the thought occurred to him that he would have to dig a healthy-sized grave. – What a beanpole the man was! Hadn't done him much good, though, had it? Into the ground he'd go, just like everyone else. –

Selivanov went down to the brook, sat down on a rock and started to clean himself up. The little stream was a trickle, blood from his face and hands coloured the water. One of the dogs came running up and began lapping at the water.

"You're drinking my blood, you she-cur!" Selivanov was just reaching for a stone when he thought again. "Drink then, frig you! Why waste it?"

The cold water made his head ring.

When a thing hurts, he thought, stepping towards the cabin, – you have to understand what it's telling you. It's life shouting about itself, that it doesn't want to leave a person. But who is it shouting to? Itself, or what? So, it's worried on its own account, then. Say I take a knife and slap resin from a tree on my wound, that's 'cos life tells me to! But isn't that life me? That's to say, I'll still exist, as far as the man who blew me away's concerned, but for myself – I won't! If there was a God, then it'd be easy to say what happens: the spirit flies off to God, and the spent case is no more use. But *there*, on the other side, you get either heaven or hell, depending how big a sinner you are. Nope! If there was a God and a heaven too, then why should people put up with their dreggy lives here, they'd all be rushing straight off to heaven, wouldn't they! But none of them's in a hurry to do it, not even them what are priests, no, they're not in a hurry neither, and they don't live too clean, what's more. That means it's not such a simple question for them either, right? –

Selivanov grinned. If there was a heaven, soon as a person found out about it he'd put a bullet in his brain there and then, the quicker to get there, 'fore his pockets got brimful of sins. What'd be the point of staying alive? –

The resin boiled on Selivanov's wound like a red-hot iron. He wrinkled his face, stretched out his neck and screwed his eyes tight shut. When he opened them, he looked again at the sky. It was just as blue and bright as before.

Course there's some kind of mystery to the sky! What doesn't have its mystery? Everything around is secrets and cunning and trickery, among men, among animals, even among stones! Why do I put resin on my forehead? To clot the blood and staunch the wound! But why? If some clever quack or other could tell you that, then you could find another question to match that answer, fit to leave the quack wringing his hands. And if no one knows the final answer in any case, what's the use of asking questions? One person may know the answer to ten questions even, and someone else a hundred, but ask the hundred-and-first question and he'll shut up – so what kind of wise man is he? Now if there was a God, now . . .

At this point Selivanov addressed a very private thought to himself: did he wish there was a God? Sensing the blasphemy inherent in the very question, he said out loud, "Course I do!" But inside his head he thought, almost without fear, that in fact he didn't wish there was a God, because without one he – Selivanov – good man or bad man, found nothing to grumble at in his life; he was satisfied with it; and after, when he'd died, there'd be nothing, good or bad. But if (God forbid!) God did exist, then his life would be measured against a quite different standard. This standard might mean that he would serve out eternity in the other world up to his neck in boiling pitch. And you couldn't escape from your torments there by kicking the bucket!

Whilst he was looking for a pine from which to take resin,

he found himself next to the officer's grave. He looked at it and was struck with wonder that the death of a good man, on whom he'd wished life with all his heart, hadn't upset him as much as that death which he'd caused himself, albeit without wanting to.

Come on, my conscience seems to have got going again now, and whichever way you look at it, it's a sin to kill! – Selivanov found it pleasurable to think in that vein. He would have liked to think of himself in some kind of special way, so as to feel both honourable and proud. But at this point his principal quality – practical efficiency – began to reassert itself; and he couldn't think any more thoughts about himself that were half-way sensible. And so in the end, he voiced a thought that was entirely lacking in wisdom, just a statement of the obvious:

"Eeh, it's hot though! He'll start to stink soon. Better get digging!"

Ivan was chopping firewood in a shirt that hung out at the back, his sleeves rolled up. Selivanov stole up to the gate and studied him for some time, unsure whether to call out. But he didn't like the way Ivan was chopping. Too damn eager by half, the way he swung the axe. Selivanov always felt an unpleasant sensation at any display of physical strength, but that wasn't it now. It was seeing Ivan play with the twenty-pound axe as if he was showing off his prowess. The chocks tumbled down on all sides under his hand, flirting to order, like a cheap tart in a bar with a client. Selivanov himself could have done the job too, but he would have been more crafty about it, divining the grain of the wood, watching and calculating, overcoming the log's resistance and obstinacy. Ivan really couldn't give a damn about craftiness; it seemed he had only to raise his hand and the log would sigh and split for him at some impossible angle.

Selivanov would have stayed by the gate but the dogs, which had gone after a cat about half a mile from the village, burst through the barely open gate, darted past Ivan's legs and pelted off behind the house. Selivanov, pretending he'd just arrived, waved to Ivan, opened the gate a crack and edged into the yard.

"What's with you there?" Ivan asked, seeing his forehead.

"Caught it on a branch, sod it!" Selivanov brushed this aside. "Well, how're you doing here? How's she?"

Ivan hedged. "Better today, yesterday was bad."

"Did she tell you about her father?"

Ivan nodded and looked sidelong at the door. "I didn't understand, who was he exactly?"

"One of them, see what I mean," Selivanov hinted, "not someone who licks the boots of the powers that be!"

Ivan frowned. "It's none of our business," he said sullenly.

"Course not, it's got nothing to do with us! Anyway, I'm taking her to Irkutsk tomorrow!"

"She's still weak . . ." Ivan said hesitantly, and Selivanov didn't like this either.

"We'll see!"

Lyudmila was sitting by the window which looked out on the rowan thicket, but then she saw Selivanov and flew towards him.

"Thank God! What's this, are you injured?"

"Just imagine how, too! Ran into a branch going along in the dark!"

"And him?"

Selivanov hung up his gun, threw down his jacket, and returned to the threshold to wipe his boots. He went up to her.

"You stop fretting about all that! Look at you, standing there shaking like a leaf! Everything's all right with him! He's going his own way, and so are we! He's gone off to Irkutsk. We walked out of the *taiga* together."

"Why didn't he call to say goodbye?" she asked, becoming wary and pale.

"Business, he said . . . Told me to send his greetings . . ."

She looked Selivanov straight in the eye and he shrank before her.

"You're not telling the truth . . . Something's happened, hasn't it?"

Selivanov clasped his hands like an old peasant woman.

"What do you want me to do, kiss the cross or something? I'm telling you, everything's fine! He's in Irkutsk, I said, gone visiting!"

The phrase was well-chosen: it changed the expression on her face, and only Selivanov's broken forehead, and his eyes that could not hold hers, stopped her from being completely reassured. Ivan, silent until then, suddenly spoke out roughly:

"Hey, come and tie up the dogs, before they trample my garden down!"

Selivanov glanced at him gratefully and hurried out, Ivan following him.

"What were you on about?"

"See, Ivan, there was someone else there too . . ."

"Well?"

"Well what! He was there, now he ain't . . . no more, not anywhere!" Selivanov answered with malice.

"Talk sense!"

Selivanov touched his forehead with his hand and looked at Ivan.

"But maybe you'd best not know it all, Vanya?"

"I'll find out all the same."

Yes, he'll go to Chekhardak and work it out for himself . . . doesn't smell of rain there . . . Blood on the grass . . . Graves . . . −

Selivanov sighed and said guiltily, "I did him in!"

Ivan grabbed him roughly by the front of his coat.

"So you haven't had enough of that yet? Not now even?"

"Don't grab at me!" Selivanov lost his temper. "I want to stay alive too, don't I! If I hadn't done for him, he'd've done for me! He wanted to take the lassie for himself, but I wouldn't let him. Got it?"

"What lassie?"

"Let go, I'm telling you! What lassie, indeed – what, got twenty of them in the house or something?"

Ivan let go and looked down at his feet, puzzled. Selivanov straightened his shirt and blew his nose.

"He gave me this cut just in passing, damn near cracked my block open. Did anyone ever stick a revolver in your face? Eh? Well, so there's no reason for you to go grabbing my coat. D'you call that fair? He grabbed me too, but once too often."

Selivanov walked into the house, Ivan behind him. Their long absence and the sight of their troubled expressions put Lyudmila on her guard again. While Selivanov washed, ate and drank his tea, she looked at him silently, waiting.

"We're going to Irkutsk tomorrow," said Selivanov. She didn't respond. It was all the same to her, wherever she was and wherever she went.

"You don't think you'll get well again in town, do you?" Ivan mumbled.

Then they tossed a few words around about this and that. Selivanov had almost completely calmed down, when Lyudmila went right up to him, so close that he had to get up from his stool, and quietly but firmly demanded, "Tell me everything!"

"There you go again!" Selivanov sighed. "You're like an old woman counting her chickens over and over. I already said . . ."

But his voice disappeared into an indistinct murmur under her gaze; he shut up, licked his lips and looked beseechingly at Ivan, who remained sitting to one side without lifting his eyes. Selivanov slumped helplessly on to the stool.

"Is he alive?" Lyudmila asked.

This was his chance: if she still hoped he was, then he could make something up to feed her hope. But his brains were like mutton in aspic.

"Come on, tell me!"

"Don't break her heart! Get on with it, if you've run out of lies!" Ivan said morosely.

Lyudmila turned quickly towards him, fear filling her face.

"He blew him away!" Ivan answered her pleading look.

"How . . . blew him away!"

"What, cat got your tongue?" Ivan growled. "Why should I do your talking?"

"Well, it's . . . ," Selivanov gabbled guiltily. "He was beating me up, he shot at me with his revolver. He shot at me, I shot at him . . . and, well . . . it was him . . . "

She made an odd little gesture with her head and went to the window. He ran after her.

"You would have gone down with him! And why? For nothing! And neither of us knows what his business was, what truth he held true? And you must go on living!"

"You're no good either . . ." she muttered too softly for Ivan to hear.

"We can judge that later!" Selivanov moved away, donned his jacket, and tossed his cap on his head.

"I've got things to do . . . I'll be back this evening . . ."

Slamming both doors as he left, he spat at the whimpering dogs and, kicking the gate with his foot, headed across the rowan thicket. He thought he was following his nose, but he soon realised that he was actually heading for somewhere, for Svetlichnaya's.

"Andrian Nikanorych!" she cried, clasping her hands. "Oh Lord! How is everything over there?"

"Got any *samogon*, woman?"

"A-a-all gone!" she groaned.

"My gullet's on fire! Have you got any, or haven't you? Well, tell me! Or I'll have to go down to the shop!"

Uttering a sob, she took him into the parlour. Selivanov tramped through the kitchen and sat down at the table, which had an embroidered table cloth on it.

"So his torment is over!" Svetlichnaya sighed.

"His is, others' isn't!"

"Did you at least put a cross on his grave for him?"

Selivanov gestured as if to say "leave me in peace". She

wiped her eyes on her apron, went to the vast sideboard and hauled out a two-litre bottle. She fetched boiled potatoes, pickled cucumbers, onion greens; she set out bread and tumblers.

"We'll drink to his memory!"

"Rest in whajamecallit!" Selivanov growled and tossed his drink back in one, without wincing. She drank too, a quarter of a tumbler. Then they chewed on their cucumbers in silence.

"What's up with your forehead?"

He waved her away.

"Where did you take the poor orphan to?"

"She's settled . . ."

He poured himself another slug, drank it down, and realised it was useless – no matter how much he drank, his heart would grow no lighter.

"Well, what if I let Ivan Ryabinin marry the lass? What then?"

What a bit of nonsense to come into his head! He expected Svetlichnaya to dismiss it with an exasperated wave – he even wanted her to; but she spoke differently.

"If they love each other, what of it? He's a good steady fellow."

"Can you imagine her marrying a peasant? His Honour's daughter? Woman, you're crazy!"

He was stung to tears. Roughly he pushed the bottle aside. "Some frigging *samogon* you've got there!"

"It's raw," Svetlichnaya readily agreed.

"That husband of yours was a *khokhol** bastard, wasn't he?"

"He was a *khokhol*," she sighed.

"Don't like *khokhol* bastards!" he said, looking for an argument.

"It takes all sorts."

"Will you marry me?" he asked, as if in passing.

She shook her head.

---

* *khokhol:* derogatory name for a Ukrainian.

"But why? We can still have children!"

She cast her eyes down.

"I'm barren . . . That's why my man left me . . . "

"How should that be!" Selivanov asked with sympathy, not concealing his disappointment.

"God knows . . ."

He seized the bottle and filled the tumblers. They drank down and started on the potatoes and cucumbers again.

"Look, you tell me. You do a person good, and then he tells you it's bad – why? Eh?"

She tilted her head to the side, making small rocking motions, and struck up a song in a thin little voice:

> I will not go to church today,
> They're marrying my sweetheart there,
> I couldn't bear it, I would cry,
> And the people would all stare . . .

"No, you tell me: I did a person good, looked death straight in the eye, and they says, 'You're no good, I say . . .'"

> The church bells have begun to ring,
> Oh! my friends, my friends, my dears,
> It's not me my love is marrying!
> How can I live a moment more?

"And someone who didn't stir a foot still gets a good name! Right?"

"Who is it that's hurt your feelings?"

"Whoever hurt my feelings should tumble to such dealings! What's the use of talking to you?"

He slumped over the table and started mumbling the words of some song, or maybe just whispering in his cups. And he fell asleep like this, at the table. There wasn't a sound from him, even when Svetlichnaya dragged him to bed, hauled off his boots and flung him down on his side. For herself, she slid

on to her bed above the stove, drew the curtain round her and
wept long in the dark.

In the morning Selivanov refused tea, slipped out of Svetlichnaya's house like a dog after a thrashing, and all but ran to
Ryabinin's. A slap in the face was waiting for him there. First
of all Ivan suggested to Lyudmila shyly that she should stay a
few more days with him. Selivanov ignored him but then
Lyudmila said, short and sharp, "I'm not leaving".

Ivan flushed with joy and Selivanov was so annoyed with
him that he lost patience; he spat, shouldered his knapsack,
gun, and set off for the *taiga* without a word of farewell.

Whilst he was away, it happened that very same morning
that a villager, passing along the path by the Ryabinin house,
caught sight of the fair-haired princess on the porch, and by
the porch the ranger standing, struck dumb and stupefied.

FOUR

Though it was quite dark now, Selivanov was still sitting on the fallen tree outside Ryabinin's house. But then his figure made a scarcely visible movement, he gave one of his sham coughs, groaned, and got reluctantly to his feet. And all of a sudden he walked off towards the house with a firm and resolute gait. In the one unboarded window glimmered the yellow light of a lamp.

Starting at the place where the gate had once been, someone had cleared the dense undergrowth of bushes and weeds, turned the earth over with a spade, and stamped it down flat so as to make a path leading to the porch. The porch too had been tidied up a little, just enough so you could use it without breaking both your legs.

Selivanov placed his ear against the door and banged on it, first with his hand, and a second time with the handle of his stick. When he heard the squeak of the inner door and footsteps approaching, he stepped back a pace and hunched himself up even more.

The door opened inwards. Selivanov gave a gasp and started back on to the top step of the porch. On the threshold stood an old man with a grey beard.

"What d'ye want?" he asked in a calm, expressionless voice.

Selivanov sniffed and made a few vague motions with his hands, but said not a word, so shocked was he by Ryabinin's appearance.

"Well?"

"Don't you recognise me, Ivan? But Vanya, it's me!" Selivanov said at last. He was agitated but spoke softly.

Ryabinin looked at him calmly. Was he casting his mind back over the past, or reluctant to recall it? It was impossible to tell. But at length he stepped back, leaving his hand on the door.

"Come in!"

Selivanov pretended he hadn't understood what Vanya had said, and waited for him to repeat it. Then he wiped his feet carefully and went through the porch into the *izba*. But when he'd crossed the threshold he again stood transfixed. Amidst the dense blackness of walls, ceiling, floor, air, a blackness so dense that the lamp was powerless to dissipate it, in the middle of all this, seeming to draw into itself all the feeble light of the oil lamp, hung, or rather floated, an icon. Now, the face on this icon was a perfect copy of the face of the man who'd let Selivanov into the house, the man who had once been Ivan Ryabinin. This was what had robbed Selivanov of the power of speech. The extent of the likeness might have been exaggerated by Selivanov in his startled state, especially since Ryabinin hadn't worn a beard before, but that there *was* a likeness was beyond question. And the black gloom of the house, which had not yet had time to seem inhabited again, appeared to contain only the lamp hanging in inky emptiness and the two faces. Selivanov began to feel uneasy, even afraid. Suddenly he made to cross himself, but half-way through seemed to recover himself and started to straighten his jacket instead. The master of the house noticed how Selivanov was fussing about in his embarrassment, but he said nothing. He was standing by the table, beside the lamp and the icon, almost as if he intended that Selivanov should catch the eerie likeness.

Ivan was wearing an open-necked shirt on to which his white beard flowed, every hair sparkling silver in the lamplight. His hair was parted in an unusual way, and the set of his shoulders, his whole stance, had something special in it. But the most striking thing was his face. It was more than calm, it was somehow other-worldly, carrying secrets which could not be spoken of or even guessed at.

"Come in!"

It was as though Ryabinin hadn't opened his mouth – his moustache and beard concealed the movement of his lips, and his voice seemed to come from somewhere behind his back. Selivanov gave a cowardly wheeze and sidled towards the table, not taking his eyes off his host; he bumped into the bench and bent down to finger it all over, just like a blind man.

"Sit down!"

Selivanov sat down obediently; there was a guilty smile on his face.

"So you're alive, are you?"

"Yes, that's it . . . I'm alive . . ." Selivanov said, almost as if it grieved him. After a pause he added, "And so are you, Vanya!"

Selivanov said the name as if he wasn't sure this really *was* Ivan Ryabinin in front of him, his friend of the *taiga*, as if he was considering the possibility that some other man had arrived in his guise, a man who might well not recognise Selivanov or know him only by reputation. But Ryabinin held his ground and looked Selivanov straight in the eye as he stood over him, and nothing in his expression betrayed his thoughts. Selivanov cast his eyes round in his discomfort.

"And your little house is alive . . ." he muttered and looked into Ryabinin's eyes with an expression of total wretchedness, just like a dog. Ryabinin said nothing but walked round the table and vanished in the darkness of the house. Selivanov didn't dare even look round. Behind his back he could hear a clatter of crockery, things being moved about; he could hear something being opened and then slammed shut again. Then Selivanov saw Ivan's hands coming from behind his shoulder as he put a tin of stew and some glasses on the table. For an instant he put a hand on the table, then laid his right hand on Selivanov's shoulder, and left it there just long enough to make Selivanov start sniffing. Shyly he touched this hand with his fingers. And for a moment everything swam as if he was on a roundabout, making him giddy with pain and joy. Selivanov sobbed unashamedly and said in a small voice, "Va-a-anya!" And his shoulder gratefully sensed the pressure of his friend's hand on it long after that hand had been taken away.

On the table plates were ready laid, and there were glittering brand-new forks and a knife, bought only a day or so ago, looking exactly like the ones in the canteen at the fur processing plant. Selivanov looked at them (too grand for hunters they were, for sure!) and pulled his half-litre bottle of vodka from his pocket. His eyes had got used to the darkness now and he could make out that everything around was clean and in its proper place. And although the house still bore signs of having been totally looted, signs crying to Heaven for vengeance (how could you hide them?), all the same there was a man in the house again now, and it had come back to life. Even with all its shutters still nailed up (except one window, that is), you could see that sight and breath had returned to it. But the damp, the smell of crawling and flying creatures, of stray cats and dogs, of earth coming through every rotten patch in the boards, mixed with the sooty smell of the lamp before the icon (Selivanov still couldn't bear to look at the way it was fixed to the wall as if it was floating in the air), all reminded him of someone's funeral (his grandfather's, maybe), a memory from early childhood buried in the furthest recesses of his mind. All this made him feel, as he poured the vodka into the glasses, that he was doing it in memory of the dead.

Shoving a glass towards Ivan, he raised his eyes and looked at him enquiringly, as if to ask whether it was all right to show him how happy he was, to express his joy in his face and in his words. Ivan crossed himself, but without fuss, as if it was the most natural thing in the world. He sat down on the bench opposite Selivanov and took the glass in his hand, but didn't pick it up; instead he stared for ages at it, or through it. And Selivanov got a good look at Ivan's fingers, which appeared to have had the tops chopped off half-way up the nails, and which were so flattened and coarse you wondered how he could bend them. It's hard work in the *taiga* too, but it never made a man's hands as ugly as that. At length they lifted their glasses and clinked them, not making a toast though (Ivan said nothing, and Selivanov wasn't sure it would be right to), and their fingers made contact, ending up side by side, Selivanov quailed before the years his friend had lived through, the paths he had walked. And Selivanov wondered why he should have had such luck. "Oh Lord," he said to himself three times, not knowing exactly why; but it meant that he was giving thanks that his fate had been as it had.

Screwing up their eyes, they drained their glasses, and munched the stew mechanically.

"Is there anything you want to know, or do you know it all already?" Selivanov asked, again afraid to look Ivan in the eyes. Funny that, his conscience was clear – more than that, he had every reason to expect Ivan to be grateful, but he couldn't look him in the eyes. It was guilt, that's what it was, like a live man feels looking at a dead man, or a successful man looking at an unsuccessful one, or a fit man looking at a cripple. But Selivanov needed an answer, so he looked Ivan full in the face and saw fear in his eyes too. Ivan was afraid to hear the truth. He could still hope if he didn't know it; and hope helps you live through anything. It can even prolong your life, though a hail of stones flies all around you. But what's truth? Fact, that's what! And it can be the last stone in the load that breaks your neck.

Ryabinin swallowed so violently that his beard jerked, and said in hollow tones, as if he felt no emotion:

"I don't know anything. Go on, tell me! But keep it short . . ."

That meant, if there's nothing good to say, don't spin it out. Selivanov got the point.

"You've got a lovely daughter, Vanya . . . and a little grandson, too."

Ryabinin's beard jerked again. His eyes, which till then had stayed calm, seemed to go away into themselves – you couldn't tell if it was joy or pain he was feeling. And in an even deeper voice he asked, "So you mean my wife . . ." Selivanov lowered his eyes, shrugged, and ran his fingers along the edge of the table.

"Tell me, then . . . but give me some more of that vodka first."

Ivan drank without waiting for Selivanov, crossed himself as if praying to God for courage, and lowered his elbows heavily on to the table.

"Go on, say it, don't torture me!"

"Well, you see, like . . ." Selivanov rushed in, leaving his glass untouched, "when you'd been taken away, that very same morning, at crack of dawn, I came along here with a cart and loaded them into it, took a few odd things as well . . . nailed up the doors and windows . . . then I went round by Piney Dale, and from there on to Irkutsk, to my auntie on my father's side. Got married in nineteen-twelve to a man working in a factory there, she did . . . I was afraid, Vanya, soon as they found out what sort your Lyudmila's father was they'd take her too . . . So I fixed them up at my auntie's, her and your little daughter, and went back myself so I could find out what was up with you. See, it was going round you'd been taken off to Irkutsk too."

"Yes, Irkutsk, that's right . . ." Ivan's beard wagged up and down.

"There now! That's just what I told her, the little silly. I says, I bet Ivan's here somewhere, bet they've stuck him in the central prison. She throws herself at my feet, says, wait a bit, please go and find out, I'm sure its my fault Vanya's in trouble! Well, where was I to go, *you* tell me, Vanya, where would they have told me anything? But then she kisses my hands, go on, she says. Well, so I go and hang round Irkutsk for a bit, then I come back and say, I've found out, he's there, they're looking into it, maybe they took him by mistake, could be they'll let him out. And you, I says, wait here a week or so, if they don't let him out, I'll be back."

Selivanov's throat had gone dry and he gave a little cough. Then he remembered the vodka, drained his glass almost to the bottom, and went on without even touching the stew: "Well, of course, Vanya, that was my mistake. You can punish me as you see fit . . . so you see, I left her at my auntie's and went off into the *taiga* for a couple of days, see, I had things to do, to hell with them, but how could I have known . . . Only, see, when I got back to Irkutsk again, Lyudmila'd gone. My auntie was all of a dither, she'd the baby there in her arms bawling its eyes out. She said she'd gone to rescue Vanya, and off she went . . . That was it . . ."

Ivan whacked his fist so hard on the table that Selivanov started up and spun round. But Ryabinin had himself in hand again, though he'd closed his eyes. Keeping them closed, he said, "Should have been another baby . . . we were hoping for a son."

Selivanov was guiltily silent.

"And my daughter?"

"Your daughter . . . she's fine, Vanya," said Selivanov quickly, relieved. "We took such care of her! She didn't want for a thing, she'll tell you so herself! Trained to be a teacher, she did, married a teacher too . . . Fine lad he is."

Selivanov made this last remark in none too certain a tone, and, seeing Vanya's questioning look, hastened to explain: "He's a good husband to her, honest to God, never raises his hand. Only thing is, he's a bit overmuch of a Party man, we don't seem to speak the same language at all."

"You mean he's a fool?"

"No, that's not the right way of putting it! You'll see for yourself. Folks round here have changed quite a bit. Life's not so hard now as it was. You can see why! After all, if one man has to slog from morning to night, the next man won't have a chance to rake anything in either. Powers that be seem to have cooled down a bit, they're not so fierce any more, so your man starts in with the songs of praise and the fanfares. And folks now, well, apart from the out-and-out idiots, they all seem sort of blind . . . You look in their eyes, and all you can see is two circles, a big one and a little one, and the little one darting about all over the place . . . but there's no life there! You could shit right in a man's eyes, and he'd still keep rabbiting on about the cult of personality!"

"Stop blethering!" Ryabinin interrupted him angrily. "Does my daughter know about me?"

Selivanov looked shifty again.

"See, Vanya, thing is you're sort of . . . enemy of the people, whatever . . . How could she have lived with it? When she was a kiddy she was always asking where her mum and dad were . . . Well, so I'd tell her her mum had got sick and died, and her dad . . . well, he'd suffered, but through no fault of his own."

Seeing the pain on Ivan's face, and his clenched fingers going white at the knuckles, he again hastened to speak. "But I never said a word against you, Ivan, she'll tell you so herself."

"How can she," groaned Ryabinin, "when she doesn't know I exist? And if I tell her who I am, how's she going to think of me, having done hard labour and all?"

"She'll think of you like I tell her to, and that's that!" Selivanov burst out. His voice had a note of arrogance.

"*You?!*"

Selivanov was discomfited.

"See, Vanya, I've spoilt her rotten. She loves me, for all I'm an old dog! I've decked her out in furs like a little queen . . . Never went to Irkutsk without taking a little something there for her! Went at it with both barrels to get her nice things! What's more, I've got sort of attached to her myself."

But there Selivanov decided he'd gone too far, and hastened to gloss over what he'd said.

"Don't you go getting jealous of me, now, Vanya! To tell the truth, I'd about given you up myself! And now I'm handing her over to you, like she was in a bandbox! We'll go soon as ever you want to. Tomorrow, if you like! Right?"

"Yes, let's," said Ivan uncertainly. "Let's have the rest of that, shall we?" Selivanov poured the remains into the glasses.

As the train bumped along, it jerked and seemed to stumble every half-mile when they went under the gantries carrying the overhead wires. The catch of the compartment door was broken, and the door slid to and fro, squeaking. People kept scurrying past the compartment; now and then someone would go into another compartment and sit down; others would move on to the next carriage. Even here in the carriage with compartments, let alone in the pullman, there was no getting away from the fuss and noise. Berry pickers carrying pouches and buckets crammed the platforms connecting the carriages and from these there emanated clouds of tobacco smoke and a hubbub of foul language and jokes that floated into the compartments.

Now and then passers-by would glance into the compartment, but seeing the two stern-faced old men in it, they would pass on. In the next compartment people were strumming on a guitar and singing trashy songs. It made it hard to think or talk.

"If you got ten years, how come you were there so long?"

Ryabinin looked out of the window and said nothing at first. "It's not so easy as that. I tried to make a break."

"A break!" Selivanov squeaked with surprise. "But why didn't you come here? Who'd ever have found you? You'd have lived like the tsar of the *taiga*!"

"Had to get here first!" Ryabinin replied morosely. "I got out three times, and every time they nabbed me in the very next village!"

Selivanov stared in amazement. He squirmed with embarrassment on his friend's behalf.

"But how could you let them nab you? Surely some people managed to make it, didn't they?"

"Yes, they did," Ryabinin sighed. "But not without shedding blood . . . And I didn't want that!"

Stung by Selivanov's uncomprehending look, he explained, "I didn't want to buy my freedom with someone else's life! But you can't see that, can you?"

"Dead right I can't! They grab a man for no reason at all and pen him up – so why not slit someone's throat to get out? I can't see it at all. No, Vanya, I'm sorry, but if you don't know how to value freedom, you got just what you deserved, you and the others. Nothing but cart-horses, the lot of you!"

He stamped his foot angrily and drummed his fingers on the little table by the window.

"What's the use of freedom," Ryabinin objected calmly, "if you lose your human nature to get it? I've seen too many turn into beasts."

"So spending half your life in that hell-hole means keeping your human nature, is that it? So what's life for, then? And why in God's name did you try to get out if you didn't want to get clean away? Wanted a longer stint, did you?"

Ryabinin frowned with annoyance.

"See, I told you, you don't understand! I couldn't bring myself to . . . Once or twice I said to myself: I'll go the whole way this time. But it didn't work! I'd get out of the zone and see a man from the village on the road and I'd know he'd run straight off and tell them, and then they'd track me down. But all the time I'd be thinking: maybe he won't tell on me, he looks human enough, so why shouldn't he have a human soul?"

Selivanov clapped his hands together.

"Can't see it, won't see it! But now tell me, hope you won't mind me mentioning it, but I noticed the first thing you did in Slyudyanka was go in the church and kiss the pope's hand. Did God help you out in that hell-hole?"

"Yes, He did," Ryabinin answered. "But I can't tell you how, not 'cos I don't have the words, but 'cos you wouldn't understand them."

Selivanov made an indignant noise in his throat.

"It wasn't you He helped, if He exists at all. It was me, 'cos I've lived out my life in freedom, and nothing's had the chance to bloody well shift me off my path! But you wouldn't risk soiling your hands for your own freedom!"

"It wasn't my hands I was worried about, it was my soul!" Ryabinin corrected him. "Who gives a toss about hands?"

"Well, your soul then! But then why didn't He help you to get out so you could take care of your soul and not lose your freedom either?"

"That's enough, Andrian!" Ryabinin begged. "We'll never agree! You've done things your way, I've done them mine. What's the use of comparisons?"

Selivanov flattened his chest on the table.

"So no regrets, then?"

"Oh yes I have!" Ryabinin sighed. "But it's more than that, there's something I understand, something different, we'll talk about it another time. Haven't the strength today! You know where we're going . . ."

The reasons why this talk had made Selivanov lose his temper weren't simple. Of course he was pleased Ryabinin was back, but with his return something had snapped in Andrian Nikanorych's life – and not only in his life, in his body too. Suddenly his lumbago had started playing him up, his hands were shaking like the alkies' down on the state farm. All this had happened at once, over hardly more than a few days. The worst of it was, he'd lost interest in the *taiga*. He'd spent a whole week getting Ivan's things in order, fixing the house and straightening out his sector, making him clothes and getting him dressed in them so that he should look like normal folks – and all this time he hadn't once thought of the *taiga*. And when he had, he'd been shaken: he felt no pull to go there at all!

So then he'd gone against his own wishes, put off the trip to Irkutsk (though till then he'd been chivvying Ivan into going – Ivan couldn't make up his mind to go and see his daughter), and he'd run off to Bald Hill in the *taiga*, where he'd been living the last few years. But whilst there he'd caught a cold, something that had never happened to him before, and even more remarkable since it was summer. And to think how he'd caught it – getting his feet a bit wet in the bog! Two days later he'd come back and spent a few days lying about in Ryabinin's house whilst the sickness had had him by the ears. He'd felt ashamed in front of Ivan. When he'd felt a bit stronger he'd rushed into the *taiga* again as if he was testing himself. He'd had some fun with the old lags at the depot, but when he got back to his cabin he realised his life in the *taiga* was over. The *taiga* had flown out of his heart and was standing some way away, all by herself.

There was something else too. Until a few days ago he'd thought of Ivan's daughter and grandchild as his own. And although he wasn't fond of her husband, the times he spent in Irkutsk were a real joy, even if he only experienced it two or three times a year. But what would they want with him now that Ivan had come back? He felt empty, hurt. And what was more, now his whole life (which he could be proud of, surely?) had been called into question and he had started asking questions, like what Ivan's God would think of it, for instance. Well, if Ivan thought God was there, even if Selivanov didn't, it still meant Ivan's God could look down on Selivanov's life from his bell-tower! Well then, and how would Selivanov's life appear to him? Selivanov was indignant. There was only one way his life *could* seem to God! After all, who had done more good – Ivan or him? Who'd saved the officer's lass? Who'd made Ivan happy? Who'd taken care of his house for him? And the sack of money which Selivanov had saved up over the years, who was going to get that now?

What good had Ivan ever done in his life? Didn't want to soil his soul, he said! But all the same he had his own God! What had he done to deserve that?

Selivanov got tangled up in his hurt feelings like a clapped out old nag in its broken harness. He'd lived all the years until Ivan vanished with a secret sense that he was better than Ivan, which had done neither harm nor good to anyone, and now it turned out that Ivan was better than he was in some ways! Even when Ivan had married the officer's daughter, even when she, the stuck-up minx, had decided not to take to Selivanov, had run her rosy pink claw down their friendship and wounded it, when that bawling baby had appeared in the house and Ivan had had no time for his friend any more – all the same the most important thing had been left. But now that his life was in its final stage, now that Selivanov was almost ready to spit on all manner of higher conduct and sing in harmony with this friend returned from the other world – now the linch-pin of his self-respect had been jolted and was no longer firmly in place. Or maybe it was another feeling that had crept into his soul – but anyway it had started to ache like his lumbago when it was going to rain.

In those far-off years, if Selivanov had thought about his old age at all he had thought that when it arrived (and how could he get away from it?) he would be rewarded by wisdom and tranquillity of heart, and would be able to see all he had lived through from above; he'd thought there would be nothing to disturb his soul. That's how he'd seen himelf, looking at his past words and deeds and all his other vanities, eyes screwed up ironically, smile of contempt on his lips. True, his old age hadn't seemed in a hurry to arrive, though years had come and gone so thick and fast he'd got bored counting them. Until the last few days he hadn't been aware of his old age at all. And then, when he had looked it in the face, it had turned out that there was no tranquillity at all, but a host of thoughts each more painful than the last, and that his heart was racked by feelings which you could have expected in a young lad still wet behind the ears, but certainly not in him, Selivanov, a man at the end of his life who'd understood everything worth understanding.

"Listen, Vanya, have you noticed, that's the third time that jerk with the camera's looked in here? What do you think he's after?"

Ryabinin shrugged without interest and kept his eyes fixed in the direction of the window. It wasn't clear whether he was looking out of it or whether he'd turned away to be alone with his thoughts.

But the young man in a sweater which wasn't right for the time of year and trousers like a tourist would wear, with a camera and a big portfolio at his side, looked into the compartment again. This time he stopped in the doorway and looked the two old men up and down.

"Excuse me, is it all right by you if I sit down here?"

"Haven't bought the seats, have we?" said Selivanov none too welcomingly. But the lad had to go and sit down beside him – at a polite distance, it was true.

"Tourist, are you?" asked Selivanov, not bothering to hide the hostile intonation.

"I'm an artist. You seemed to be having a pretty serious talk. I wasn't sure whether to disturb you . . ."

Ryabinin cast his eyes over the man and turned away again.

"Please excuse me . . ." the artist continued uncertainly, directing his words to Ryabinin, "I'm an artist, you see . . . I need models . . . what I mean to say is, er, if it's all right by you I'd like to do your portrait."

"Vanya, just listen to this!" Selivanov shrieked at Ryabinin in his surprise.

Ryabinin shrugged and looked at the lad. He too was startled.

"What do you want with me?"

"You have, er, how shall I put it . . . a very individual face . . . real find for an artist . . ."

"Find, eh!" Selivanov shouted enviously. Sensing this envy, the artist hastened to explain so as to avert unpleasantness.

"Well, of course every human being is an individual, but you see what I need for my work is specific types."

"Draw him, then, if you like the look of him!" Selivanov interrupted. "Let's see whether you notice everything you should!"

The artist hurriedly opened his portfolio and took out clean sheets of paper and a bit of cardboard to lean on, found two pencils and started using the sharper one to sketch a few crooked lines on the page. He tensed his hands as the train jerked and bounced about. Selivanov had turned away in order to show that these ridiculous carryings-on didn't interest him in the least. But a strange kind of unease made it impossible for him to seem indifferent. Now and then he would fix his eyes on the pencil as it ran to and fro across the paper; but he'd moved too far away to see exactly what was going on.

"Will you tell a daft old man why you should have picked on him of all people?"

"Well, you see, I haven't just drawn him, I've drawn lots of other people as well!" The artist was about to reach into his portfolio, but Selivanov waved him away.

"It's your business who else you've drawn! What I want to know is what it is about *him* got you interested? It's his beard, is it?"

"That too!" said the artist with a smile. "In the past they used to paint saints looking like that . . ."

"Hear this, Ivan, you've joined the saints now!"

And Selivanov burst into nervous peals of laughter. Ryabinin wasn't exactly embarrassed, but he felt uncomfortable and looked askance at the artist.

"Like the way he looks, do you, then?" Selivanov hissed spitefully. "Would you like me to tell you where he got his looks from?"

"Andrian!" Ryabinin rebuked him.

"It's all right, I'll say no more! It's just that . . ."

But the lad had stopped drawing. He cast a questioning look at Selivanov and then fixed his eyes on his model. Then he said musingly:

"My grandfather on my mother's side . . . well, he got his looks from *there* too, as you put it. But he looked quite different. He had a beard too, but there was fear under it."

"And what can you see under *his* beard?" asked Selivanov viciously.

121

"I'm not sure now," the lad responded quietly, looking at his sheet of paper. "But when I came in I was . . ."

"Let me tell you, lad," Selivanov announced proudly, "we're not like your grandad, we're not that sort of shit at all. We can scare the life out of anybody, we can!"

"Why should you be like him?" the artist objected. "My grandfather was a Communist from the beginning! He fought with the Red gangs and took part in the collectivisation campaign! But when he got back from *there* he was scared out of his wits, and then he died . . . of fright, more or less. I'm not condemning him, of course, you couldn't say it was a holiday camp."

"Don't believe you can draw at all!" announced Selivanov in categorical tones.

"Why don't you believe me? You haven't seen, have you?"

"Show us you can, then! Get on with it, we'll be in Irkutsk before long!"

Just then a small fat woman of about fifty in a man's jacket, a shirt which looked as if it might have been made from an army greatcoat, and gumboots, shoved her way into the compartment, pressing against her stomach a basket with an aspen leaf on top which seemed to be full of berries. Selivanov greeted her in fairly welcoming tones, but she put down her basket and sat down with an air of recovering property which had been unlawfully appropriated by someone else. She cast a hostile look round with watery eyes, pursed her lips and started to stare at a point between Selivanov and the artist. The train jerked forward.

"Brute! You'd think he was driving cattle, not people!" she muttered angrily.

"Been collecting a few berries, have you, lady?" asked Selivanov in oily tones.

"What else! To hell with them!" the woman answered truculently.

"Well, no one made you, did they?"

She frowned.

"Ask me that when you've tried living on my wages!"

Her eyes started to look even redder and more watery.

"Look, this is an artist we've got here," Selivanov nodded in the lad's direction. "Would you like him to draw your pretty face, then?"

"Living off the fat of the land must make folks go bloody barmy!" she snapped, turning her back, offended.

The artist looked at her with surprise, then at Selivanov, then back at her again.

"What do you mean? It's my job!"

"Job indeed!" the woman hissed with contempt. "Just you try standing at a counter for ten hours weighing out three tons of potatoes! Just you try having anyone who feels like it calling you names as if you were a dog! You try getting home and finding your useless bastard of a husband pissed as a rat again and having to clean him up!"

"You should throw him out and find a job that isn't so tough!" Selivanov tactlessly advised.

"You silly old fool!" she yelled, beginning to sob. "It's men like you drive us women into our graves before our time! We should do away with you all, you useless bastards!"

"What's all this racket for?" said Ryabinin calmly. "Everyone has their own troubles."

"Well, what's yours, then?"

But she took one look at Ryabinin's face and subsided. Sniffing, she fell silent. No one else said a word either until the Angara appeared at the window shining like mica. The train was getting in to Irkutsk. Without saying goodbye to anyone the woman shoved her way out of the compartment, balancing the basket on her stomach.

"Well, show us what you've been scribbling, then!"

"I haven't had time to finish," muttered the artist.

"Eh! We aren't having any of that! Show us!" Selivanov demanded.

Ryabinin was looking towards the paper too. Selivanov took the drawing and his face darkened. It was Ivan, you could see that. But it looked even more like the saint whose icon was in Ryabinin's house. Selivanov suddenly felt sick. Without showing Ivan the drawing, he shoved it back at the artist.

"Take your scribble away!"

The lad shrugged.

"Thank you! Goodbye!" he said coldly and slipped out of the compartment.

"No point in showing it to you!" Selivanov explained sourly. "Else you'll start feeling your shoulder-blades to see if you've got wings there!" He shook his head. "Just fancy! Hardly out of nappies, shit for brains, but what he can do with his hands! How a man's hands can be cleverer than his head I can't think, but there it is! But tell me this, Ivan, will you: why are people so attached to their horse-collars? Take that woman who was in here just now: why does she put up with that man of hers and with back-breaking work? I'd hang myself! How can you bear life when it's unbearable? Her life's so bad it's turned her into a she-wolf, but she won't let go of her horse-collar! Take a look at them all, Vanya; they're all as spiteful as wolves, but they go on and on ploughing, and never even lash out with their hooves! Wild beasts've got more sense than that, they go looking for somewhere better. They tear the throats out of anyone who does them wrong. Even a hare, for instance, that's a shy creature, but if a kite grabs him in open country he'll flop over on his back and he may even manage to tear the kite's guts out with his claws! But what's gone wrong with people? They're far worse than wolves among themselves, but when the wolves are around they're much bigger cowards than hares."

"We're here." Ivan got up and took the suitcase off the rack.

Selivanov sighed and got to his feet too. They were the last to get off.

"Are we getting a tram?"

"Have you gone round the bend?" said Selivanov with morose pride. "Think I've spent my whole life rushing round the *taiga* so I can ride on that rattle-box?" And he dragged Ryabinin off to the taxi-rank.

"Where do you want to go, grandads?" asked the taxi driver, a cheerful young lad.

"Ushakovka direction!" replied Selivanov grandly, sprawling over the seat. Ryabinin squinted at the meter as if it was a baby snake making straight for him, and made himself comfortable too, but the taxi driver put on a vicious turn of speed, and he was flung back on to the seat.

"Gently now, gently! No need to belt!" grumbled Selivanov.

As they crossed the Angara bridge they had a view over Irkutsk. Ivan sighed, but without regret.

"You'd never recognise the place!"

"They've smartened it up all right!" Selivanov agreed. "Just look at the clothes people wear now! And to think you didn't want to wear your suit! You'd have given your whole family the fright of their lives if you'd turned up in the clothes you had on before!"

"I'll give them the fright of their lives anyway!"

"Don't worry, Vanya!" Selivanov reassured him. "You're visiting your own daughter. A father's always a father, after all! Blood's thicker than water, it always has the last word!"

"All the same I can't help worrying!" Ryabinin sighed, sinking his fingers in his beard.

"Long time since you've seen your daughter, is it?" asked the driver, not turning round, but meeting Ryabinin's eyes in the mirror.

"Good while, yes," Ryabinin answered reluctantly.

"Fair enough! These things happen."

"Understand a lot, don't you?" Selivanov sneered.

"Not much there to understand! You're not the first I've had by a long chalk! I've had plenty with more to say for themselves, so of course I know what's what!"

"Tell you anything interesting, did they, the talkative ones?"

"We don't pass on other people's conversations!" said the driver meaningfully, winking at Ryabinin in the mirror. "So which are you? A 'high-up' or a plain one?"

"What?"

"He's asking you whether you're an ordinary bloke or one of them in their star-studded uniforms!" Selivanov explained. "He's an ordinary bloke!"

"Right! Were there a lot of you there?"

"Aren't you interested in how many of them still are there?"

The driver turned right round and looked at Ryabinin, astonished.

"What do you mean? Surely they let them all out? When the cult was denounced?"

"Look 'ere!" Selivanov gave a satisfied wheeze. "Here's another one with shit for brains! So you thought you'd been handed truth and justice on a plate, did you? Turn right here! We're going to the new blocks!"

The driver spun the wheel and sped forward into a sea of mud, bouncing over hidden potholes. Ryabinin saw his face in the mirror. It was wearing a sombre expression.

"It's the second block, last entrance!"

When Selivanov was paying, the driver asked, "Are you going in for long or shall I pick you up when you tell me? I can do that for you . . ."

Selivanov was touched.

"Thanks, mate! Problem is, I don't know myself, depends how things turn out."

"Were you there too?"

Selivanov made a rude sign at him.

Right by the door Ivan tugged at Selivanov's sleeve.

"Hang on! I must get my breath back. Listen, maybe you'd better go in by yourself at first, tell them what's what . . ."

"Fine!" Selivanov said savagely. "What's what, eh: like, 'scuse me, it's your dad outside the door, could you let him in the house please?"

"You don't understand . . ."

"I understand anything God meant folks to understand! My understanding's enough for me! The point is, *you* should understand. You've done no one any wrong, but just show me which of us has done no wrong to you! Come on!" And he pressed the bell.

They'd taken a long saw, set to perfection, and sawed a man along his length, and what was left was only half a man.

If Ivan had known how things would turn out, he'd hardly have had the law on that swine with the thick eyebrows, would he? To hell with him! He should have let him shoot as much as he'd wanted and then clear off back to town. Then none of this would have happened . . . None of this would have happened? Just think of that, none of this would have happened! When you thought of it you wanted to howl like a wild beast, lower your head and charge, smash everything round you to smithereens! But you couldn't butt anything, couldn't smash anything. You could only howl, but softly, and shake your head about, and use your nails to scratch your shaven head . . .

He'd nabbed a poacher in the *taiga*. It wasn't the first time in his job, but it was the last. He'd turned out to be a high-ranker! So they'd "stitched Ivan up", made out he was a terrorist, mixed up with the gang. Ivan had yelled in a terrible voice in the court-room about truth and justice, it was shameful: a great strapping man, bawling away, eyes like saucers. It had been hard to tell whether he was going to tear everyone to pieces, or fall on his knees and beg for mercy . . . It could have been either, but he didn't get the chance. They were in a hurry.

They'd sawn a man in half, they'd sawn his soul in half in the day of his prime, of his happiness. And Ivan had rent his shirt and had told himself sternly that he'd had it coming, that he'd been too happy, had more than his share! No wonder he hadn't been able to believe his own happiness for ages, that he'd woken up night after night and lit a candle so that he could see his wife's face on the pillow next to him, so he could check she was really there, that he hadn't dreamt it.

The first year he was shut up he'd counted every day. It had felt as though his life had ended. After that he'd just been aware of the anniversaries: what had happened on that day two, three, four years ago. How in such-and-such a year on this very same day at such-and-such a time Selivanov had come into the house, and how SHE had been following behind him. And how on this very day and at the very same time as he was sitting here now in this transit cell he'd said to her in his clumsy way that maybe she'd fancy spending a little more time at his place. And how later, at the very hour they were now having the evening roll-call, she'd told him he was a good man! And how four years ago that very night . . . God! Had it really happened? Better that it never had! If only someone would tell him, even as a joke, that it had never happened, that none of it had ever been, that he had invented it all, that all his life, from birth till now, the boundaries of the camp zone had been his horizon, and that all the rest was a dream!

But everyone, whoever you talked to, was in the same boat, and they were all cut in half, half-people wandering round together and tearing each other apart with their griefs.

And how many of them there were! You would go from one place to another, and then another, and everywhere more people, and barbed wire round them all! God! Were any of them left out there, on the other side? Did the other side even exist? Was the whole earth covered by the squares and circles of fences and boundaries?

But no! Through the cracks in the transit van you could see life. But didn't that make it even harder, even more painful?

And then there were the smells! That was what had induced Ivan to make his first break and get his stint doubled. He'd been considered a quiet man. A guard had been taking him on his own through the wood, and suddenly there'd been a rowan tree on the path, and he'd been struck full in the face by the familiar smell. His head had spun, he'd stopped breathing, there'd been a mist before his eyes. He'd flung himself at the screw, snatched away the rifle, snapped it in two on a tree

128

trunk and run for it . . . And run and run . . . until he reached the next zone.

And how many times after that, especially at night, he'd suddenly felt familiar scents stealing on him: scents of home, of the *taiga*, but most sickening of all – the scent of a woman's body! And his sight had been blotted out by the shadow of his brows, he'd bitten his hands in order to stop himself sinking in the whirlpool.

He'd never dreamt when he was free. But there dreams came to him, and always about the most important and secret things in his life. Sometimes he'd dream that he was walking down a footpath in the *taiga*, when suddenly he stumbled across a length of barbed wire, and when he tried to get round it he found it went on for ever – running through trees, tree-stumps and cliffs and stretching across his whole life. Sometimes he dreamed he was trying to kiss his wife, but his lips started trembling uncontrollably; or that he was trying to leave the house, but the street door was locked, the windows had bars on them, and there was a hole in the door for food. Or that he was taking aim at a bear, but the barrel of his gun turned into a rag, and he couldn't run away, his legs had turned to lead.

These were dreams of fear. But there were also dreams of tears. He'd suddenly find himself leaping into the air off the roof of the hut and flying up over the zone and away from it, and the roof on the watch-tower stopped the guard from shooting, and the guard howled with rage, knowing that he wouldn't get his extra leave now. Or he'd suddenly find, when he knelt down beside the bunk to find something which had fallen down under it, that there was a hidden tunnel there, so he'd go down into it and walk for ages and then get to a flight of steps and end up in the cellar of his house in Ryabinovka, lift up the trapdoor with his hands and see the joyful face of his wife and his little baby daughter pointing her finger at him.

He'd wake up in tears and feel no contempt for himself because of them.

How many years had passed since his former life had started

129

to float away from him like a puff of grey smoke, and then turned to a mist, then a frost-covered window, until finally it seemed as though it had never been his life at all, but someone else's, a life which occasionally made him groan inwardly, but for which he felt no pain! That was when his soul started to be born anew. Now and again, among the other men and sub-men he would meet people from another world, and he was drawn to them, drawn to their calm and their inexpressible wisdom. And he accepted the Verity of what they believed, not with his reason or perception, but with his feelings. The frozen glass melted away, and a new world without end or boundary opened up before him, without beginning or end, and every man behind him in that world was reflected only in his good qualities and in that which unites all men. All around him were people explaining things, discussing things, angry people and those who were broken-spirited. Before, he'd tried to understand them in the context of his own fate, but each of them had his own language and his own words, and their fates were different, and all of them were strange to him. But now each of them turned out to share his misfortune and suffering, and became his brother in consolation and help.

The path of Ivan Ryabinin did not run smooth even after he'd found his faith. There were disruptions, doubts seized hold of him, he was suffocated by attacks of despair. At such times he would break out with demonic strength and commit wild and idiotic acts. And how could that not happen when a man's human essence had been raped, his soul and flesh defiled, when his very human self had been corrupted by the force of injustice! But afterwards, when he came to himself, his soul would be lit by such pure light and would illuminate all the darkness which was still to come.

But he never came to terms with his loss of freedom, never. Not with a single word did he bless it. Although he understood that he had acquired new vision by grace, he knew that the reason he had stood in need of this was not that he had enjoyed abundance or a happy life. No man can bless the pain of the knife opening up a septic wound so that his life may be saved. That was why he had tried to escape. It wasn't that he hoped to get out or get back; he tried to get out precisely because he was afraid of getting used to his lack of freedom. He wasn't afraid of the length of his sentence, he was afraid of forgetting his real self, his human self, born for freedom.

He took the first extension of his sentence as an irrevocable misfortune. The second made him heave a heavy sigh. The third left him unmoved. But when the chief of all the camp chiefs died and they started to release the innocent, and none of this applied to him because he'd run away and had not been resigned to his fate, that was when the hardest year began, a year which nearly made him destroy the faith within him by laying hands on himself in his despair. But then, when he came to himself again, he found that ordinary life with its hopes and dreams had left him, and he turned his inner eye to that life which is the only real truth, the very truth about everything and on every subject. The words of prayers took on new meanings for him, and every word had such weight in it that when he spoke it he spoke not one word but a thousand. His soul had burst into new bloom, and the joys of the world, of which the loss of his freedom had deprived him, were experienced by him over and over, to the full, all the more so because by at last renouncing external life he had opened his eyes to the life which had been unheard and unseen in him. He recognised his own arrogance and the joy it had suppressed in him. When you realise for the first time what it is like to experience simplicity of heart, even if only for a minute, then you begin to see that arrogance is as disfiguring as a hunched back. Yes, truly it is like a hunched back, for if it is cast out for good every fibre in a man's body cries out against the severance.

One day, without giving it any special thought, and without trace of hypocrisy, he suddenly took and forgave someone who'd done him wrong. He'd forgiven people in the past, but not without entering what he'd done on to a mental register, like a work quota fulfilled. And now he suddenly felt, not that he'd done his duty to God by forgiving, but that the offence itself had vanished as if it had never been there. It wasn't a grave offence, but that wasn't the point! The point was that there was light in his soul. It was like a breath of fresh air coming into the musty atmosphere of a cell after a storm. And later he forgot the offence and the offender, but he seemed to freeze and to attain a new state of still and joyful peace. It was as if he had entered a house so tiny you could see right round it, but which, once he was inside, had turned out to be a huge and beautiful palace, with endless chambers, staircases and halls. And when the voices of vanity called him out again and he returned and looked at the house once more from the perspective of a vain worldly life, then he trembled in his heart because he had known its secret: inside it was larger than the whole world in which he had lived and suffered until then. The most important truth had been revealed to him. The world of human joy is not wide compared with all the griefs which a man's fate can bring him. But a man has only to find his way to joy, overcoming the hazards of that path each time anew, and he will see the light of another world.

How much effort he had wasted before on fretting about others: how not to offend a kind man, how not to provoke a vicious one, how to keep a stranger at bay and how to stay in contact with a loved one! People had seemed so hard to understand and so unwilling to understand in their turn. You had to live with them and settle down with them, get used to them. He'd experienced cold and hunger, and bribery and corruption – what *hadn't* he suffered! – but the biggest hurts had been inflicted by other people. It's people who make captivity terrible, he'd thought until not long ago. But now everything had changed. What had happened was that he seemed to have stopped thinking about the people round him, that is, he'd stopped guessing, he simply accepted them now for what they were, without bothering about his opinion of them. He'd stopped making mistakes. More than that: he couldn't tell how it had happened, but it turned out there were

more good people than bad round him. And then their attitude
to him had changed. It wasn't because he was older now that
they'd started calling him "dad" or "father" more often, or
even by his name and patronymic. And he hardly seemed to
know his patronymic himself; he only ever remembered it at
the official roll-calls, or so it seemed to him.

The day of his liberation took him by surprise, though he
knew when it was to be. Disquiet stole into his heart on the
morning of that day; then, as he was called out to the watch,
as he said goodbye to his fellows, grieving for them, as the last
forms were filled up, his disquiet grew, turned to outright
worry; and then to confusion when he found himself beyond
the checkpoint and roads opened up before him on all sides,
leading nowhere and to no purpose.

Should he go to Ryabinovka? Was there anything left of
home? He thought of Selivanov; it was a long time since he'd
done that. He'd taken a good look at each new lot of convicts
during his first year in the camp, because somehow he was
convinced that Selivanov could not escape losing his liberty
either. He'd somehow got the idea that Selivanov wouldn't be
able to stand that fate and was certain to waste away; so in
time he felt as though he'd buried his friend, thought of him
as if he were dead.

But now it crossed his mind that Selivanov might have
survived after all, for he was very sly and crafty.

His wife, his daughter, the child who was due to be born
and who must be in the prime of life by now – he didn't think
of them at all, or tried not to. And was it his fault if even they
had become strange to him since, as far as they were concerned,
he was forgotten thrice over, dead and buried, and their
new life separated them from him like a wrought-iron fence
separating a graveyard from the world? No, he didn't want to
go back to the woman who had been his wife, whether she
wanted him or not. What for? The three springs they'd spent
together, those three logs, part of the frame of a whole house
– hadn't they sunk under the earth, subsided under the weight

of years of separation? They wouldn't stand up! Now his daughter and son, that was different (or maybe it was another daughter). But there was no sense in thinking of that at all.

To Ryabinovka, then? Whether to Ryabinovka or anywhere else, it was all the same to Ivan. But he did go to Ryabinovka, because he couldn't think of any other place where he could go.

A man of about thirty opened the door. Seeing Selivanov, he greeted him warmly, like an old friend.

"Natasha!" he called. "It's Andrian Nikanorych! Come and say hallo!"

Ryabinin's heart responded to the name "Natasha" rather belatedly. – My God! My daughter! The thought flashed into his head, and he was taken by surprise as if until now he hadn't believed in this meeting.

"I've got a friend with me today," Selivanov warned, shoving Ivan forward.

"Come in, we're glad to see you both!" the young man answered. He studied Ryabinin curiously, and Ivan was not unaffected by this scrutiny.

A young woman, still almost a girl, rushed up to Selivanov and hugged him tight. Then she caught sight of Ryabinin, was disconcerted and greeted him politely.

"This is my old mate Ivan Mikhailovich!"

"Fancy that now!" Natasha clapped her hands. "An old friend, and we've never met him before. How come?"

"Haven't seen him in ages myself!" Selivanov replied. "But now I want you to love him and make him feel at home!"

"What are we standing in the doorway for? Come in! But Andrian Nikanorych, you led us up the garden path! When did you say you were coming?"

"Didn't work out that way!"

Ryabinin had never seen Selivanov like this. What was it about him that was new, he wondered. And then he answered his own question: it wasn't he, Ryabinin, who was the father of this beautiful young woman, it was Selivanov. Natalya didn't look like her mother, or only a very little. But she reminded Ryabinin very much of someone else.

"Eh, Vanya, she's your spitting image!" said Selivanov as if he'd read his thoughts. And Ryabinin was afraid he wouldn't stay dry-eyed for long.

"And where's our little grandson?" Selivanov asked.

"Running round all over the place!" the young man answered.

Whose grandson? Mine, does he mean? Or is he saying it's his? Oh God, did I come here for nothing? They're better off without me! It's too soon! Too soon!

They went into the living room, which was not very large. The table there had been set. They live well, then, Ryabinin thought, looking round. The things they've thought up now! If you tried putting that furniture in an *izba* in the country it'd look silly, but here it's right. Looks nice.

He ran his eyes over the walls, the furniture, squinted at the window, and all to avoid meeting the eyes of his daughter. He could feel her looking at him, sense her curiosity. Curiosity, yes, and that was all! Just as well, he thought, that she's not too like her mother. She could have been the dead spit of her . . . how would I have coped then? He made a deliberate effort to think about something else, so as to stay calm, but he could hardly stop his hands from shaking. Somewhere inside him a kind of painful trembling was stealing up to his heart, and when it got there he was sure he wouldn't be able to hold back the tears.

"Sasha love, will you run and get the baby, now?"

"Why should I run? He'll be here soon enough by himself!"

When Natasha had gone out to the kitchen, Selivanov seized his chance. He took her husband by the sleeve and whispered to him:

"Ar, look, don't get me wrong, like, but do you think you could go out for a little walk? See, we need to have a little talk with Natalya! We'll let you in on the secret soon! Run along now, be a good boy, don't take offence!"

"What do you mean, talk? Course I can go out, if that's what you want!"

"Well, go on then. Aha! We won't keep anything from you, but we need to be private for now . . . And take the mite with you, so as to give us a bit more time. We need to have a serious talk."

Natasha's husband shrugged and put on his jacket. He had adopted an expression of indifference, but he made a bad job of hiding how surprised and hurt he was. He shuffled his feet and muttered, "Well, I'll be off then!"

"Right, right!" Selivanov hurried him, hearing Natalya's footsteps.

"Where are you off to?"

"To get the baby!" Selivanov reassured her. And as soon as he heard the click of the lock, he took Natalya by the shoulders and sat her down in the chair opposite Ivan.

"We're going to have a talk, Natalya! No, just you sit there! You must sit down for this kind of talk! For the moment at least . . . You'll jump up soon enough, just you see!"

And now Ryabinin heard the sadness in his friend's voice for the first time. He's handing over his fatherhood to me! But do I have a right to it?

"Well, you see, Natasha, daughter . . ."

Selivanov got stuck on this word and blinked in his distress.

"You see, lovey, I call you my daughter because . . . that's how things turned out . . . see, you've been like a daughter to me, so you have . . ."

"What on earth are you on about, Andrian Nikanorych!" Natalya could stand it no longer. Selivanov's voice shook so much it was painful. Ryabinin too gave a little cough, his throat was so tight.

"What was your maiden name . . . do you remember?"

She looked at him with surprise, but went all tense at the same time, as if she suspected she was going to hear something painful, something she didn't want to hear.

"Ryabinina, you know that very well yourself!"

136

"See!" Selivanov sighed. "And that man sitting right opposite you is Ivan Mikhailovich Ryabinin, and he's your very own father! So, now you know."

She moved her eyes to Ryabinin very slowly, and he dropped his eyes like a guilty man, a criminal.

"Is it true?" she asked softly.

He lifted his eyes. He knew there were tears in them, but too bad! He wiped them away with his sleeve and nodded.

Selivanov picked up his chair, turned it round, coughed gently and said, "You just sit there and look at him! And in a minute I'll tell you all about your father and your mother, and your grandfather, I'll tell you all the things about your life you never needed to know before!"

FIVE

Although the next morning was a Monday, the train turned out to be packed to the doors with people out to forage for berries and nuts, with hunters and with fishermen. Scarcely a quarter of those among the noisy, colourful crowd were supposed to be having the day off. And because the great majority had come at their own risk – had employed every ounce of their cunning, sharpwittedness and resourcefulness in order to find a way of skiving – there was an atmosphere of wickedness and mischievous jollity, and everyone seemed a little feverish. People were thirsting to be sociable; they were guffawing, bustling about in disorganised throngs and apologising to one another without stopping. They smoked incessantly, singeing one another's hair and flicking the ash to land on the backs of other people's heads or right on the crowns of the smallest ones. There were more men than women, but where the women, especially the young ones, had gathered together, the jollity overflowed all bounds, bursting out through the wide-open broken windows giving on to the platforms between the carriages.

There was no ill-will, no swearing, no abuse. All that would come on the way back, when the sated, overtired, disillusioned crowd was hurtling back to town, into the grip of their tedious everyday routines.

For both Selivanov and Ryabinin crowds in general, let alone ones as rowdy as this, were like all the torments of Hell rolled into one. Ryabinin had grown unused to them, and

Selivanov had never been able to stand people treading on his toes and stopping him from seeing anything. But the fact was, Selivanov couldn't face being alone with Ivan at the moment. He was fed up to the back teeth with him. It'd been God's own job getting him to stay the night, and in the morning it'd been impossible to keep him there a minute longer. Their departure had been extremely embarrassing and painful.

Selivanov was bursting with pity for Natalya, but at the same time he despised himself for feeling like this – it was so unnecessary. Why should he worry his head over Ivan's carry-ons, after all! You see, the thing was, Ivan thought that the whole business had been a mistake, that he'd never have anything to say to his daughter. She'll never have any daughterly feelings for me, he'd said, I'll just be a burden to her. The truth was, Selivanov was both sorry for Natalya and cross with her too. He didn't see it the same way she did, he thought. She'd turned to stone, just sat there with tears pouring down her face and a stony look. And that husband of hers, the bastard, you should have seen his eyes nearly drop out of his head when he heard where his father-in-law'd just got back from. Sat there yammering on about "reerbilitation"! You should've seen how Ivan's eyebrows shot right up into his hair. And as for the grandson, no matter how Selivanov'd tried to get him to go up to Ivan, well he just wouldn't, stood there squinting and dribbling, refusing to budge.

What's more, Selivanov felt sorry for Ivan too, all at the same time, so the upshot was, the whole thing had ended in tears all round, and maybe Ivan was right, maybe he should have stayed in the background at first, had a good look at them, and only later made up his mind whether to tell them or not.

But in all honesty: why *had* Selivanov been in such a hurry? Wasn't it because he wanted to give Ivan back what he was due as quickly as he possibly could – he couldn't stand it a minute more, he was nearly biting his fingers to the bone. And what had happened now? He didn't seem to have managed to give anything back to Ivan, and yet he hadn't kept anything for himself either, had he?

They couldn't squeeze into the carriage itself, so they staked out a little corner for themselves by the door of the platform, leaning their arms on the metal panelling of the door and holding the crush off them with their arched backs. You could see in every inch of Selivanov how angry he was with Ivan. But Ivan didn't even notice, so wrapped up was he in his own thoughts. He looked sad, and there was something pathetic about the sight of him in his crumpled and ill-fitting new suit. The cuffs of his white shirt poking out of the sleeves made his hands look even coarser, more yellowed and wrinkled.

Looks older than I do, Selivanov thought unhappily, but without pity; the thought popped into his head, that was all. – Just look what we've come to! Him caged up, me free, but we've both got old just the same. – No, that wasn't a right thing to think, not a just thing. Selivanov wanted to think about Ivan, not with pity (bugger that!) but with understanding for his fate, his peculiar fate, not the fate of every man. Selivanov couldn't even imagine what would have happened to him if he'd had Ivan's fate. The very thought of it made him shake all over!

Selivanov saw Ivan's beard jerk and guessed he was saying something. He leaned right across to him, with his face almost in Ivan's beard so that he could hear the words above the din.

"What I'm saying is, now if I'd been let out right away, a year later, and I'd turned up and found myself with my wife gone and a little baby to look after, I'd have gone right to pieces! It'd have been the death of me!"

Whenever Ivan started to justify his fate like this, Selivanov ground his teeth. It sounded like an old woman, not a man, all this blessing one's fate and crossing oneself! He couldn't believe his ears when he heard such namby-pamby muck from Ivan!

"Course you wouldn't have gone to pieces!" he yelled into

Ivan's beard. "You'd have been off your head with grief for a while, then you'd have pulled yourself together. Life must go on."

Ivan shook his head.

"But you saw what she was like, my Lyudmila! Like the dawn! All that time I lived with her, I could never believe she was mine, that she wouldn't go and leave me! Every time she went out of the door I'd look through the window to check she wasn't going through the gate. You're a single man, how can you know what it's like to have a lovely wife, the first years you're together specially, when it's all kisses and roses? And then suddenly – she's gone! Into thin air! And it's someone else's fault!"

He shook his head again.

"I'd have gone to pieces, I tell you! If she'd gone off by herself, maybe I'd have been all right. Knew she was too good for the likes of me! But when it was someone else's fault . . ."

"And I tell you you'd have pulled through! Pulled through, I say!" shouted Selivanov, shouldering aside some man who was trying to squeeze between him and Ivan. "Who do you think you're shoving!" he shouted angrily.

"Keep your hair on, grandad!" the man responded, squirming backwards. "See that sexpot over there with her bucket, trying to get her hands on all I've got!"

"All you've got, indeed!" responded a woman shrilly – no spring chicken, by her voice. "Have a hard enough time getting the bleeding tom-cat I live with to leave me alone!"

The men round about guffawed, and Selivanov waited impatiently for them to quieten down.

"She didn't like me, your Lyudmila, you know, though I never did her nothing but good turns."

The taunt flung by Selivanov at Ivan was an old one, due for airing long ago, but he spoke without wanting to offend. He just had to say it, that was all. Selivanov desperately wanted Ivan to tell him he was wrong, contradict him. But Ivan just nodded morosely.

"You never can tell how their minds work! She couldn't forgive you for blowing her little friend away!"

"Little friend, my foot!" Selivanov raged. "One hell of a friend he was, I don't think!"

Ivan shrugged, and Selivanov, swallowing his renewed feeling of pique, turned away, pursing his lips.

Half-way back, the platform began to empty. People got down at the various halts and wandered off in different directions. Everyone knew a special place for finding mushrooms or berries, which they naturally kept a close secret. And it wasn't long before you could find a place in the carriages to sit down. So Selivanov duly went off to search for one, leaving Ryabinin standing on the platform. A minute later he came back looking pleased.

"That's enough of wearing ourselves out. Let's go and sit down!"

They sat down on the very edge of their seats, one opposite the other, knees touching.

"No, no," Ivan went on, as if their previous talk had only just been interrupted. "She bore you no ill-will. And she was grateful, believe me she was!"

Selivanov waved his hand as if to say, enough of that, I know it all anyway, let God be her judge! And inside he wondered how she'd ended her life. Had she suffered a lot? Surely she couldn't have had as much to bear as Ivan? After all, she was no peasant woman, with her grand background and all!

"Here, Ivan, what was her maiden name? I only ever knew her father's name and patronymic! Never asked his surname, it was sort of awkward."

"She had a posh surname, one of those aristocratic ones. Told me herself there were hardly a dozen names like it in the whole of Russia. Obolensky, that's what she was called."

"What did you say? Obolensky!"

Selivanov froze. Something was biting him.

"Never heard a name like that? But I have, when I was in the camps, and all sorts of other ones as well, from all of them ex-s."

"But I *have* heard that kind of name before . . ." Selivanov said. He sounded scared, and said not another word until they arrived at Piney Dale.

It had been arranged that morning that they were going straight over to Ivan's, but when they got to Piney Dale Selivanov suddenly took it into his head to go to Luchikha. He'd remembered something he had to do there. Ivan gave him a good-natured grin: he remembered his friend's passion for secrets from the old days. When they said goodbye, he laid his hand on Selivanov's shoulder, giving him a soft, affectionate look.

"Here, thanks for everything!" His voice shook.

"Haven't done anything really," Selivanov said, embarrassed. In the past Ivan hadn't exactly over-indulged him with such displays of cordiality.

"I mean, thanks for my daughter and everything. I'm in your debt, you know!"

"Vanya! What on earth are you talking about!" Selivanov pleaded, feeling his body tremble and his eyes grow wet. Ivan looked at him thoughtfully.

"I've never been able to work you out . . . You're a queer fellow, and no mistake! Were you maybe fibbing to me just now, how you don't believe in God and that?"

Baffled, Selivanov shrugged.

"You can't not believe! Or why are you doing good, then?" Ryabinin continued, more to himself than to Selivanov. "If non-believers do good, they only do it for their own ends."

"Well, *I* do it for my own ends!" muttered Selivanov. He found Ivan's speculations painful.

Ivan shook his beard with conviction.

"It's not true! Don't believe you! If you aren't a believer, you must have God's image inside you all the same somewhere!"

"Oh, leave that alone! Or have you forgotten maybe how many people I've sent off to your God in my time? I'm a killer, you said so yourself, or have you forgotten?"

"Course I haven't," said Ivan, "that's why I can't make you out!"

"Shut it, Vanya! Can't stand this sort of talk!" It pained him the way Ivan had started to natter on in his old age. "Right, time you got your bus now. I'll go with you as far as the stop. You can expect me back by evening, I'll drop in then. Don't forget to feed the dogs now, will you! They're pining for the *taiga*, don't like being tied up."

"Yes, I'll feed them. But let's visit the *taiga* tomorrow. It's high time! At first I didn't feel like it, but now I've got to."

"Any time you like, Vanya, any time! Load of crap you were giving me before about how you didn't feel at home there! You just have to get the smell in your lungs! Run along now, there's your bus!"

Selivanov went along to where the road forked and the path to Luchikha began, and Ivan went off for his bus, which was just coming round the bend.

There were lots of Ryabinovka people in the bus, and they all had a good look at Ivan. The younger ones did it openly, bold as brass, the older ones sneaked a look on the sly, but they were even more inquisitive. There wasn't a free seat anywhere. But then suddenly there was, next to a bent old woman.

"Good day to ye, Ivan!" she said as he sat down beside her. "Don't know who I am, do ye?"

Ryabinin looked closely at her.

"Well, if it isn't Svetlichnaya!"

She gave a bitter sigh.

"I made that young hussy get up so I could talk to you. You'd think they'd have the manners to do so without being asked! So, what good things did you see, Ivan, when you were far away?"

He was taken aback by her question. Surely she knew perfectly well where he'd been? Was it a slip of the tongue? No, it wasn't. Svetlichnaya wanted to know what *good* could come out of being in such an *evil* place.

"Don't really know what to tell you . . ."

It was true, it really wasn't easy to tell her. Good things?! Not even one, measured by the yardstick of human happiness.

"Ye-e-es!" she drawled, as if she understood how hard it was for him to speak. "But you're not bitter, are you?"

"I don't know," he answered honestly. "Sometimes I think I'm not, and then again, sometimes I feel . . . well, not bitter maybe, but none too good either."

"But you found God there, didn't you?"

"How do you know?"

"I can see it."

He looked at her with curiosity.

"I'm coming from the church now, in Slyudyanka. The father there was giving us a sermon, he says to us how we must look after the *taiga*, not light bonfires there for nothing, because the *taiga*'s a gift from God to man for his own good! He was saying about how people being greedy spoils the *taiga* . . . He's a good father, he is!"

Ryabinin nodded. Yes, all this was far from simple for him. He'd got used to feeling God's presence by prayer and by exercising his own will, and he was scared of the church. It felt close and stifling there. But more than anything he was scared of hearing the priest say something crooked and untrue, scared of feeling offended on God's behalf if he witnessed impurity in a sacred spot. Now when he was on his own with an icon, he was used to that: an icon was pure and holy – on it the image of God had been imprinted by God's grace!

The icon he had hanging in his house now had been given to him by a certain martyr of the faith who had cherished it and kept it hidden for several years, as Ivan himself had in his turn cherished it and hidden it later – not for long, it's true, since he'd got out only a year after. There's a law, an unwritten law, that it's forbidden to take anything away with you to freedom which would do more good inside. But the elder had commanded him to save the icon, for people had been telling tales and there was a search out for it in all the secret places there were. And there aren't so many of those in a camp . . . A guard had been bribed to get the icon out from behind the barbed wire, and then Ryabinin had taken it away.

"Vanya, tell me this," Svetlichnaya whispered into his jacket. "You've seen and heard more than I have, so tell me, is this power set up over us now the Antichrist, or not? We're told all power is granted by God . . . But this one?"

"What do you think?" was all Ryabinin could find to say.

"You can understand it in different ways! At first it was clear enough, or seemed so: it was a mutiny against God. But then again, if that really is it, it's been going on a long time now, so you can't say if it's a mutiny or a new sort of power. Father at the church doesn't tell us anything about that! Raise not your voices against the Lord, he says, your fate is in His hands. But suppose the Antichrist has already spread his wings and cleaned his beak, and God has drawn his sword in readiness for the Day of Judgement! O Lord, grant that we may die in time!"

"Don't worry, you will!" Ryabinin gave a wry smile. "Can't tell you whether it *is* the Antichrist or not, but whatever happens, these times we're in will last a fair while! Better say, God grant that our grandchildren may understand what's what!"

But at that instant he remembered his own little grandson, who'd taken fright at the very sight of him. And nothing about the baby, nor his parents, nor about a single thing in their world suggested to Ivan Ryabinin that his own grandchild was destined to understand the most important mystery known to man. But there again, who could guess the paths things might take? They were beyond all knowing.

"What's that you're saying?" He'd missed something Svetlichnaya was telling him.

"I was talking to you about your friend Andrian. He looked after that house of yours for you. Waited for you night and day. He's a troubled man, help him!"

Ryabinin said nothing, probably because he wasn't so sure that Selivanov really did need help. And also because, although he'd found faith in the one Verity beyond all doubt, he wasn't sure that he was any firmer on his feet than was his "troubled" friend. Slippery old Selivanov didn't seem to have got bent in his old age, if anything he'd got taller – that, at any rate, was how Ryabinin saw it.

"How've things been with you?" he asked Svetlichnaya.

She snapped her lashless eyelids together, moved her desiccated lips, shrugged her bony shoulder and looked guiltily at Ryabinin.

"I don't know . . . Hardly seemed to notice! What sort of life do you think a single woman has? Besides, I'm not living in the wood, I've got people all round me, so there's always things to do. Maybe you and Andrian'll visit me some day? He used to come over now and then, you know, though he's such a loner. He was terribly cut up over how he let your wife go! I knew her too, you know, before you did herself. And her father . . ."

"I know," Ryabinin answered. "You're a good woman, Svetlichnaya! Come and visit me too, I'll always be pleased to see you!"

The village came in sight and the Ryabinovka dwellers shoved their way to the exit. Ryabinin and Svetlichnaya also got to their feet. He took her heavy bag for her and walked her all the way home, adjusting his pace to her uncertain elderly footsteps. But he declined her invitation to go in and hurried off back home through the rowan grove.

From the dense mass of the forest nearby exciting, disturbing sounds and smells floated over to him. He knew now why he had not gone rushing into the *taiga*, why he had contented himself with squinting at it from the side of the porch which overlooked it, not even taking a proper look, holding himself back, as it were. Now he knew! The fact was, he was no longer sure of himself, his legs, his hands, which for so many years hadn't held a gun, his eyes – who knew what his sight was like now, it hadn't been put to the test, after all. And what could be more terrible than to be unfit for work in the *taiga*!

And only now, though his fears remained, did he feel an irresistible pull to his former haunts, to the half-forgotten paths and deserted cabins. In his first years of captivity he'd spent countless nights wandering the *taiga*, covering endless ground in his imaginary walks along the familiar *taiga* paths, recalling every bend, every tree, each stone at the bend, every stream, and every single pebble at its bottom.

All the way to his house he walked with his eyes fixed on the *taiga*; it even gave him a stiff neck. "Tomorrow!" he decided, once and for all. And he fed the dogs as was necessary the day before serious work in the *taiga*, and talked to them, promising them as much freedom as they could possibly want. And the dogs understood, and in their excitement ate little.

Never before had Selivanov been seen in Luchikha in such a fancy outfit. He had a suit, a white shirt and even proper lace-up shoes on. Acquaintances who greeted him (and, come to that, who *didn't* know him in Luchikha) widened or narrowed their eyes depending on temperament, looked after him when he had gone, and, if there were two of them or more, exchanged glances. After all, how had Selivanov usually looked when he was seen around in the last few years? Tattered old clothes, a stick, wheezing and groaning for all he was worth. They'd known perfectly well he was putting it on, but they'd got used to him doing it. And now here he was swanking around the village like a young lad, dressed up to the nines as if he was going to a wedding, not a sign of a stick, and such a haughty expression it fair made your blood run cold!

Selivanov was perfectly aware of the impression he was making on other people, but he only grinned happily to himself and immediately forgot all about it, for his head was almost splitting with such complicated things, it felt as if his skull would burst open at the neck.

What could all this be? he was thinking. – Surely Ivan

148

Ryabinin couldn't expect more torment from heaven? Surely he'd suffered enough? Spare him this one, he thought sincerely. But his desire to know the truth was just as sincere.

Now what could he remember about the lad he'd rushed to Luchikha to get hold of? He'd turned up at the farm processing plant about five years ago, and in the first week he'd worked there he hadn't come to work sober once, so Selivanov had heard. They'd wanted to sack him, but at first they didn't have a replacement, and later they'd found out that he was good at dealing with the lump of twisted metal which went by the name of the processing plant tractor, and realised that intoxication was the boy's normal working state. On the whole the lad had turned out malleable and biddable, and he didn't get too aggressive when drunk, though even when he'd first arrived he'd been missing half his teeth, knocked out in brawls. As for the bruises he always had on his face, those he got from the tractor. He had a rare talent for bashing his head into something at least once a day, and when the tractor was playing him up and he had to dive into its innards, his filthy curses, directed at the magneto or whatever, would drown the sound of the tractor's engine. He would come in to the light again with a black eye or with an angry purple bump on his forehead. He wasn't a boy at all, he was a nasty little woodlouse! As for Selivanov, he didn't think of the boy as any kind of living creature, but as an appendage to the tractor, the more so since both tractor and driver lived on the same fuel.

Everyone thought of him as "that layabout" or "the daft fool off the tractor", and no one had any idea where he lived or how he lived or where he had come from, and no one wanted to know either. No one ever called him by his name – they would just say, "Where's that lad off the tractor?" and the answer would be, "Crashed out behind the tractor!"

His face always wore a silly smile and there was a gleam of lust for vodka in his eyes. It seemed the only thing he bothered about in life was where his next drink was coming from. And he couldn't talk about anything for long without mentioning how much he'd "put away larse night", and how it would be no bad thing to get hold of a bit more. He worked just as much as he had to so as to keep himself in drink. When he wasn't working, he was always asleep. And if there wasn't work for him at the processing plant and he was out of booze then he would go round drumming up custom, that is he would belt round in the tractor from village to village, offering to collect and deliver stuff, to plough, to get rid of weeds or simply give people a ride.

Always in rags and always covered in motor oil, he was a walking joke. Selivanov himself had only had dealings with him once, and it had ended with the silly moron shooting his finger off with Selivanov's small gun. The tractor driver's surname was a joke too: it was Obolensky. When he found out the impression this made on people, especially strangers from outside the village – *dacha* dwellers, tourists and the like – he started introducing himself to everyone without being asked. But now his surname spelled anguish for Ivan Ryabinin.

Selivanov's timing was perfect. The tractor was standing on the grass plot opposite the office, and Obolensky was sprawling on the grass beside it. When he saw Selivanov, he staggered to his feet.

"Selivanych! Are you getting married, or what?"

"Where are you off to?" Selivanov asked briskly.

"Nowhere for the moment. Why?"

His eyes widened – there was booze in this somewhere. Selivanov squatted down beside him. Obolensky had the alkie's calling card, a permanent stench of alcohol on his breath. Selivanov wrinkled his nose.

"I've got work for you!"

"That'll be half a jar!" the tractor driver responded immediately.

"You can have as many jars as you want!"

"Nope! Jar first, talk after!"

"Suppose I wrap the jar round your neck?" Selivanov diplomatically observed.

"E-e-eh!" Obolensky moved a little further away. "Tisn't public property, you know!"

"What's your name?"

"Mine? It's Vanka. Why do you want to know?"

Selivanov held his breath for a moment, screwed up his eyes, and with them still closed, continued:

"And what was the name you got from your dad?"

"E-e-eh!" responded Obolensky, surprised. "Ivanych!"

"And where do your parents live, then?"

"Get on with you! What're you pestering me for? I'm from the children's home. Get to the point and gimme the jar!"

"You're coming with me," Selivanov said, getting to his feet and stretching his legs to make the blood flow back into them.

"Where're we going?"

"First of all to wherever you live. You can get changed and have a wash. This is a clean job."

Obolensky was dumb with astonishment, then he bawled: "No-ope! You want me to nick something! Over my dead body!"

Selivanov looked him up and down contemptuously.

"Nick, my foot! You need brains for that!"

"And you've too much brains for your own good!" Obolensky flared up. "Get to the point, no need for all these big secrets!"

"This is the point. You need to be clean for this. We have to give a bloke some help. You think anyone's going to let you in the house looking like that?"

"But the tractor?" Obolensky couldn't take this in at all.

Selivanov didn't go into the hut where Obolensky was living. He sat down on a fallen tree-trunk and waited for the young cretin to get himself looking decent, if there was any chance of him doing so.

His thoughts, each one sadder than the last, ebbed and flowed like slow waves breaking on a beach. Maybe it wasn't the right thing he was doing? Would any good come of it? Would it just cause Ivan needless pain? And when you thought how fate had treated Ivan already! And for no reason! And what about Ivan's God? What had happened to his vaunted wisdom towards humanity? If this had happened to him, Selivanov, that would have been one thing. But Ivan . . . was that really just? Maybe it wasn't right . . .

Selivanov got off the fallen trunk. A minute more and he would have abandoned the whole business, but just then Obolensky appeared. He was in crumpled but clean shirt and trousers. But he looked no better, even though he had washed and gone so far as to comb his hair. He was clearly feeling ill at ease; he hadn't managed to get his hands clean, and he didn't know where to put them. Only the irresistible urge to get his hands on a "jar" could have forced him to do such violence to himself.

"We're going to Ryabinovka!" Selivanov said.

"But what about the tractor?"

Obolensky couldn't imagine himself without it.

"We're going to see a man there," Selivanov went on. "And for every filthy word you let out of your mouth while we're there, you'll get a whack from me after! You hear?"

Obolensky looked sulky.

"But if you don't swear once, and don't talk crap, I'll buy your drinks for a week."

At this, Obolensky looked brighter, but doubts and worry still showed in his face. They walked in silence to where the path for Ryabinovka left the main track, about a mile away. Together they walked the whole way to Ryabinovka in silence too, and in silence they visited the village general stores, where Selivanov bought one bottle, reducing Obolensky to gloomy disappointment. Then they walked the length of the village to Ryabinin's house.

"We've got things to do," Selivanov responded curtly to Ivan's enquiring look. "Get us a bite to eat with this, will you."

Selivanov poured a full glass for Obolensky, and a very little for himself and Ivan. They drained their glasses and munched in silence. Selivanov couldn't make up his mind to start speaking. He was squinting at Ivan and fidgeting.

"Right, so tell us what your name and patronymic are, will you?"

"To hell with me patronymic!" the boy retorted rudely but cheerfully.

"Answer my question, will you! Have some respect for your elders!"

"Ivan Ivanych! Eeech!"

Obolensky was genuinely amused at introducing himself by name and patronymic.

"And your surname, so what's that, damn you? Bloody boy's got water on the brain!"

"Obolensky, if you must know!"

Selivanov glanced at Ivan and saw his lips go white and his eyes deaden.

"So you don't remember your Mum and Dad?"

"I told you – I'm from the kids' home!"

"And what place of birth have you got down in your passport?"

"Irkutsk, only I've never been there. The home was in Zalari, and me course was in Cheremkhovo, and then they sent me here . . ."

He looked longingly at the unfinished bottle, but Selivanov pretended not to notice.

"Been boozing long?"

"Mind your own business! I buy it with me own money, honest money. Does no one any harm!"

"I'm asking you when you started drinking!"

Selivanov's tone was disagreeable, and Obolensky squirmed under his glance, not even looking in Ryabinin's direction.

"They drank in the home," he answered timidly.

"What, all of them?"

"Well, not all of them . . ." and Obolensky lost his temper. "What are you cross-questioning me for? Get to the point!"

"Let's go!" Selivanov got up and they went out into the yard. Selivanov looked round.

"See the logs over there? They're in the wrong place. Ought

to be dragged right over to the fence there so the wind doesn't blow the whole pile over. There's a litre for you on me if you do the job!"

Obolensky was so taken aback his mouth fell open.

"What're you on about, Selivanych, eh? Why did you make me have a wash, then?"

"Mind your own business!" Selivanov yelled. "If you want the litre, you'll do as you're damn well told!"

He went back into the *izba*. Ryabinin was sitting holding his head in his hands. When Selivanov sat down beside him Ivan lifted his head and asked softly.

"Andrian, surely it can't be true?"

"Well, Vanya, you see how things are. I had a good look at him today. He looks like his mother. His face has gone to the bad 'cos of the pig's life he's been leading, but all the same he looks like her. Only thing is, why did she register him in her own name? But then again, I s'pose yours would've been even worse: enemy of the people and all that . . ." Selivanov shook his head. "What a life we've both had, eh! When I think of bowing my head and giving thanks for it! Well, Vanya, all I can imagine is, if your God really is just, he'll have to send another flood to end it, because it's not a life at all, it's a damn disgrace. When the war came there were those as was whingeing about divine punishment . . . And even then I knew it wasn't man's job to judge this life, 'cos it's not made by human hands!"

He looked angrily at the icon above Ivan's head.

"Well, Vanya, but what can you do? Can men really be made to be like men again? Can men's breeding really have vanished for good?"

"Maybe it's a mistake?" Ivan said in a tone of utter hopelessness and waved the idea away himself. "Can I really have found my son? And if I have, all the same he *is* my son! He'll have to be told!"

"Take your time. It wouldn't be good to do it all at once. You've seen for yourself he's an alkie . . . It'd be as well to try and get him off the bottle first."

"Hang on!" Ryabinin said shakily. "But how old is he? What year was he born? How old should he be now? Twenty-five, is that it?"

Selivanov shoved back his stool with a tremendous clatter and darted out into the yard. Smeared again with resin and dirt from the birch-bark, Obolensky was dragging the logs over from one fence to the other and stacking them any old how.

"Hey, you! What year were you born?"

"Eh?"

"How old are you, I'm asking?"

"Twenty-five, so what?"

"Never you mind! A toddler could make a better job of those logs!"

Selivanov went back inside and slammed the door. He sat down beside Ivan again.

"So it is him."

"It's got to be, Vanya!"

"What's he doing out there?"

"Shifting logs about."

Ivan put his elbows on the table and straightened up.

"For better or worse – he's my son! So we must tell him!"

"Take your time, I'm telling you. Why don't you go off into the *taiga* for now, and I'll have a go at him, see if I can knock some sense into his silly head. Breeding like that can't vanish altogether!"

"But surely . . ." Ivan hesitated.

"Listen to what I'm telling you," Selivanov broke in. "Whatever you think you've got to give the lad some warning!"

"Let's go and have another look at him!"

"Come on, then," Selivanov replied, rising to his feet.

The log-pile which Obolensky had been stacking was such a hideous mess that Selivanov could not stop himself from spitting.

"Will you look at that mare's nest!"

But suddenly he gave Ivan a frightened look. This was the lad's father, after all! He'd better keep a rein on his tongue.

But it was hard to see what this oaf could have in common with Ivan and his beard, let alone with Ivan's wife – graceful as a swan she'd been, as far as Selivanov could remember – or with his grandad the officer (the very thought was shameful!) And would the Irkutsk lot accept him as a relation? Fine brother and sister they'd ended up! With luck the log-pile wouldn't fall to bits while he was dragging those last ones over . . . But Selivanov realised that it was bound to. Just two or three goes more, and it would all come tumbling down for sure.

"OK! That's enough!" he shouted, his anger sounding in his voice. "You've done it! Enough, I said! Leave those ones, there, will you!"

Obolensky shrugged, looking at the old men with astonishment. Ivan stepped down from the porch and went up to him, looking sad and stern.

"Thank you!"

"Didn't do it for no thank yous! What d'ye think I am, a performing bear, to be fobbed off with that!"

Ivan went on looking at him just as sadly, and the boy looked a little cast down.

"Don't need to, I'd 'ave done it anyway – how much work d'ye think there is in dragging a few logs around?"

His tone was none too sincere, but Selivanov could see that Ivan's look had melted. Even his stance had relaxed. Well, after all, why *should* the lad drag other people's logs around?

"Thank you!" said Ivan again and went into the *izba*. As he passed Selivanov, he gave him a rather guilty look.

Selivanov pulled a ten-rouble note out of his pocket and gave it to Obolensky.

"How much are you giving me there?" Obolensky said, breathing heavily.

"A tenner."

"What, a whole tenner? For three logs?"

"Well, how much are you asking?"

The lad spat and swore.

"Piss off . . . I don't need anything. What're you trying to hide? Force me to wash . . . Now you give me a tenner for three logs. What d'ye want me to do?"

Selivanov was a bit stumped for an answer to this.

"See now! There's a good man living alone here! He once spent twenty-five for no good reason at all. Keep an eye out, he may need firewood, or some other thing. Take a look when you roll by on the tractor."

"Why didn't you say so straight off?" Obolensky, reassured, crackled his ten roubles. "Course I can. I'm in Ryabinovka once a month or so, and with the tractor. The old man'll be OK! What's all this about twenty-five, though?" he said doubtfully.

"Go on," Selivanov waved him away. "When your throat's dry, come back to me, I'll wet it for you."

"Eeh, piss off!" Obolensky broke into a smile of satisfaction. "But you do come up with the goods, I'll say that for you, even if they all say you're a miser!"

"They say! Let their tongues wag! Now be off with ye!"

And he took him round by the well and out.

Ryabinin went into the *taiga* on his own. All Selivanov's attempts to put him off were in vain: he *would* go to his old sector, though he knew it was no longer as it had been: high-tension cables were being stretched through its very heart, the wild beasts were gone, and an open wound had been slashed through not only paths and undergrowth, but brooks and springs too! Even the breeze carried the stench of machines on it.

He walked in a dream, as he had dreamt in that hateful camp sleep when night offered no rest, only torment. Now, as then, he felt as though he were certain to wake up at the moment when he was ten paces from one of his cabins, or when he shouldered his gun to aim at a quarry, or when his heart filled with joy at finding some familiar place. The sensation of sleep was so strong that Ryabinin would sometimes stop in his tracks and say something out loud, so that he could hear his own voice. But even then his voice sounded to him as if it were coming from another person, just like in a dream; and each time he would shake his head, surprised, and go on. He would stop rooted to the spot if he suddenly recognised a rock or – even more miraculous! a tree stump (after God knows how many years!); on the other hand, he would all but break into a run when he realised that here there was a turn in the path coming up to left or right, that here there was a bit of a slope up or down; and when everything was indeed just as he expected, he would say to himself, "Aha! Oh look! I remember!" He frowned if he came across an unexpected fork in the path. That meant a newer path had been trodden out since he was away. That was bad: he felt jealousy stir against the stranger who had been here without him, as if the stranger had no right to be there.

Then he couldn't find one spring; then another. Vanished . . . It happens in the *taiga*. Others had turned up in their stead, but he didn't drink from these. He strained his ears to all the voices of the *taiga* – now *they* hadn't changed in any way – and he recognised them all, calling by name each and every creature that gave voice.

It was the very beginning, the first days of autumn, and the mature trees in the *taiga* were still untouched by the season; the grass was only just losing its lushness in one or two glades; but the sultry heat had passed, the sky was no longer so brilliant, and everything living and growing was, not drowsy exactly, but full of repose and quiet contemplation, the feeling you get when, at last, after prolonged and mighty efforts, the moment you have been waiting for arrives, and you can look round placidly and benevolently and say to yourself, "It's not so bad after all. And I'm not so bad after all either. And, who knows, there may be good things and happiness still ahead."

Ryabinin's former sector was not under Siberian pines. On the knolls Scots pines predominated, on the heights were larches in tatters from being eaten away by the larch miner, and a jumble of branches and leaves filled the hollows. It was only along the streams that Siberian pines and oaks as big as two or even three span round the middle, many with wind-damaged crowns, broke the enveloping blanket of saxifrage. The boughs were heavy with pinecones. No blow from an axe would have made any impression on these pines; the branches wouldn't even have trembled from the impact. So they were left in peace, and the cones hung until the first frosts and the first strong wind brought them down (if a nutcracker didn't fly up and peck them off, of course). When the wind blew, the cones fell into the snow and were preserved until the spring, bounty for squirrels and chipmunks, and for passing hunters too – who can resist munching nuts in springtime?

Capercaillie had always used to rest up in the oak woods at midday. Without thinking about it, from sheer ingrained habit, Ryabinin went to one of their haunts and loosed off a shot from Selivanov's Sauer. But the silence did not explode with the whistle and clatter of capercaillie wings; only a chipmunk squeaked somewhere along the rocks by the brook. The sector was empty.

Ryabinin scrambled round the sandy bar by the edge of the brook – he didn't turn up a single spoor. Beyond the brook his one-time sector began. With his first steps in it, he realised he'd made a mistake; he should have listened to Selivanov and not come out here. Even before he ran into a cigarette box on the path and then the remains of a campfire with all sorts of rubbish around it, Ryabinin's thoughts had left the *taiga* and returned to everything he'd hoped to shelter from in the twilight, if only for a few days. A daughter, a grandson . . . and a son. How had it come to this? What was to be done? How should his life be now? He turned it first this way, then that, in his mind, until finally his head spun with thoughts. Why couldn't he make up his mind! Why the confusion? Perhaps he should go back, go to the church in Slyudyanka, then go on a strict fast? Rationally he already knew that this was exactly what he must do; but the minute he realised it he started walking again, head hung low. And then everything pressed in on him at once: the way men had debauched the forest; the weariness of his legs; the noise of the machines over the rise; a pain in his back; the looting of the cabin; the tree stumps for fifty paces all round. His throat was seized by thirst, and his tongue stuck to the roof of his mouth.

That little stream which he had once lovingly edged with stone: had it dried up, or been trampled into the ground? A weak flow seeped out from under a tussock, and the water stank like a stagnant bog. Everywhere lay tins, paper, rags and all manner of human filth. But worse even than that: some degenerate species of human had got hold of an axe and slashed the trees, one by one, out of hatred for beauty and freedom; those that were still standing bore the scars of the hooligan's flailing. The *taiga*, defenceless, disfigured, quietly wept its tears of resin.

Ryabinin stood at the threshold of his cabin and cast his eyes over the vandalised stove, the smashed bunks, the knocked-out windows; then stepped back, straining his ears to the noise of machines over the rise. He'd had a cabin over there, too, a low hut dug into the earth with turf walls. That was where Selivanov, wanting to score one off him, had once carved up a Manchurian deer and got caught at it; and from there Ryabinin had chased after him and taken a charge of shot in his thigh. The same leg was grumbling now, but not from the shot.

He went down to the old spring again, cupped a palm to wet his lips, and walked towards the machines – he wanted to see with his own eyes what man's will had wrought, as if he'd decided to subject himself to torture. He emerged at the summit of the rise and could already see the cutting extending like an arrow to the horizon, repulsive in its straightness, looking like a slash made with a sharp scythe – right across the spine. But his heart held no indignation, only grief. Directly below him two bulldozers were crawling into the blind cutting, letting out ear-splitting howls, like hungry curs gone wild. Not a single human was in sight, which made the iron dogs seem even more awesome.

Ryabinin went towards them. The louder the roar became, the harder he clenched his teeth, until his cheekbones ached.

He emerged in the blind cutting itself. Seeing him, the machine-operators were mute. They were only kids, snotty-nosed machine-bred little kids, born in the stench of fuel oil, raised in the clamour of diesel engines – and dedicated to machines in the service of mankind. Because mankind cannot now take a single step without the aid of a machine.

When the kids came up to Ryabinin, surprised, but pleased, they felt like sons to him. And this was indeed a miracle; he, who hadn't been able to feel for Obolensky as his own flesh and blood (or so he thought), suddenly sensed kinship with these rascals, other people's sons. He wanted to do something nice for them, say something kind, as he had neither done nor said to his own son; but as he didn't know what to do or say, he just stood there smiling.

"'Ere, take a look at that!" one exclaimed. He was thick-set and square-featured, and grinned broadly to show strong teeth with big gaps between. "Where did you spring from, grandad?"

"From Ryabinovka. And you?"

"Well, we're from Tunka. We're pushing through a high-tension power line. Twenty miles already!" The lad looked round at his mates and said admiringly, "Quite something, this grandad, ain't he, lads!"

Another, the senior among them by the look of it, stretched out a hand to Ryabinin.

"Stepped out of a fairy story, have you, grandad?"

"Right first time!" Ryabin said, shaking the oily hand. He wanted to add, "God forbid *you* yourself should ever end up in a fairy story like that," but what was the use?

"This was once my sector," he said, casting a glance at the neighbouring rises. "I made my living out here . . ."

"So now your living's up the spout," said one of the lads,

all sympathy. "Will you be from the little hut down there by any chance, over the hill?"

"I am from there."

"Well, we're moving over that way today, and our last quarters are a fair long way behind. Listen, grandad – make us some grub, well y'know – heat up some tins of stew and we'll come and have us a banquet together. We've got some booze to set us on fire. You can tell us a fairytale! We finish early today; we've over-fulfilled the plan, and as you know, that deserves a bit of a party!" Without waiting for a reply, he shouted: "Genka, will you bring that stew over here!"

Ryabinin more than agreed with the plan; he was delighted. And when they'd squashed the tins of food into his rucksack, and hung their mess-tins on the straps, he went boldly back, clanking and rattling, to the vandalised cabin, forgetting his weariness and the ache in his back, though it had a fair load on it. Ryabinin knew now what he wanted from these oil-streaked lads: to ask them about his son. No matter that they didn't know him; he would ask them what he would have liked to ask his son. He could relax with them. They were alive, weren't they – so they must have something that gave them a zest for life. They had minds, so they must have thoughts; they had parents who loved them.

This last thought set him shivering. Would he have to learn how to love as a parent? He had loved many people in his time, but that love wouldn't do for his son, nor for his daughter and grandson, not even for Selivanov. He loved God too. True, he'd always loved Him with his mind, in any case, but now from time to time this love would turn into a feeling so strong that the memory alone would suffice him for months, making him tremble with the joy of what he'd lived through.

And his son? An alcoholic, practically an idiot. Must he love him? But how? The word "son" whirled round in his head in a circle, and couldn't seem to break out of the circle to enter his heart.

And his daughter? The word had long been in his heart and

had never abandoned him; that was why he felt such pain and hurt, and still other feelings which wouldn't bear examination. Thin threads stretched to him and away from him; they were weak, they tangled at the first touch and broke, so that he had to unravel them and tie them together again. And all this work caused him so much tension and confusion! Lord, what a heavy burden it is! Forgive me, Lord, it was easier *there*!

Ryabinin knew this thought was sinful, and wrong in its essence. It could never be that a man in his right mind would find it easier to be in a state of humiliation and bondage. But how much confusion there was now! It wasn't like that *there*!

How had he thought things would be, when he was *there*? Well, he'd taken it for granted that his torment would finish when his time did, that the joys of freedom would be his reward. But it took wisdom to be able to accept joy calmly. Could that really be how it was? He felt no resentment against God, only this confusion . . . but then again, what is confusion if not resentment?

The first thing was to gather firewood, then erect a crosspiece on which to hang the mess tins of water over the bonfire laid ready to light, so that it would take just the strike of a match. He busied himself with the cabin, hauling away so much junk of all sorts from indoors he felt quite sick! The bunk had to be repaired, but he'd only brought the little hatchet with a rubber handle along; fat lot of use that was for chopping! But chop with it he did, refashioning and strengthening the struts under the bunk. He blocked up one window with birch bark to stop the draught. He couldn't re-hang the door, the hinges were rusted through, but he cut grooves in the doorway so as to slot the door on the inside; a house without a door is no kind of home! Whilst he was at work, he fancied he might even put up a new cabin some other summer, spacious and light. They'd make their cutting, string along their power line, and then . . . they'd leave. The game would come back. And though there'd be a scar on the *taiga*, a scar never killed anyone.

The cabin he'd build would be big enough for his whole family to live in during the summer. Could anyone really grow up normal who wasn't reared in the air of the *taiga*? It heals you, that air, and makes you young again, and fills you with tranquillity and seriousness.

Ryabinin started to call to mind all the most beautiful places in the sector: it needed somewhere with both a spring and dry ground, and a good pine wood. That's where he'd build his cabin. He pondered how to lay a trail for a horse there, so it'd be quicker getting bricks to build the stove, and the other materials he'd need. If you fell lumber for a hut in the forest, better do it at least half a mile away from where you're building, so it looks like the cabin's grown out of the roots of the trees round it, without a single stump to rend the eye! It's nice to have two or three grassy glades alongside, where you can cut hay for your horses and to feed the game in the forest, yes, and then you always have that scent of hay near the cabin which is such a joy to the heart. He would get some of the puppies from Selivanov's bitch . . .

Selivanov again! Ryabinin was always putting off thinking about him because he needed to think long and hard. But if he didn't think too long about it, then wasn't it for his sake the Lord had spared Selivanov – Selivanov, his only kindred spirit? He was ashamed to think it, but surely it wasn't possible that without God's will one person should stay loyal for twenty-five years, even when he thought the other was no longer in the land of the living! There was nothing he could do to make amends to Selivanov. His own excessive dryness and stiffness of behaviour saddened him, but was it his fault if he felt more surprise than joy at what Selivanov had done? He'd always wanted to understand him, when instead of understanding he should have been trying to take him to his heart. If he'd swapped fates with Selivanov, how would he have lived then?

It was a prickly thought. He wondered: if they'd taken

Selivanov then, instead of him – and there'd been reason enough to, after all – would he have washed his hands of him? He'd criticised Selivanov then; even now he didn't approve of his behaviour, though he no longer sat in judgement on him. Why exactly had Selivanov stuck by him? No reason!

Ryabinin shut his eyes, stood straight, and as he'd done in the days when it had been impossible to make the sign of the cross openly and pray out loud, said in his mind the words that signified thanks to God for everything that had come to pass.

When he opened his eyes, his head spun and for a moment his heart did not beat true. "I'm tired!" he thought, listening to the rumble of machinery down in the cutting. When it died down he'd have to kindle the fire. It wouldn't take long to heat up the stew . . . They'd come, and it would be ready.

But the thought of the moment when he'd have to kindle the fire filled him with anxiety, because he knew what the smell of it would bring back to him. Although he'd lit more than one fire during those years, and they'd been enough like *taiga* fires to stir and taunt him, yet he knew the semblance was empty. A fire in the *taiga* has its own specific aroma, and he'd never forgotten it, like many other smells in his life.

On a nearby stump a nutcracker perched and cawed, rapping the cracked and yellowed cut in the stump with its long beak, fluttering its wings. "You ninny!" Ryabinin said, "Lost your way, or what? There's nothing for you here! Fly away to the hollow, you'll find pine and oak trees enough there!" He waved his arm, the nutcracker flew off, and after making a semicricle over the glade, vanished into the pines.

The human tongue is not adapted to the voices of the *taiga*. You can practise, of course, and do violence to your throat, but you'll be far from mimicking all the sounds of the forest. This had interested Ryabinin since his youth. A bird's got a voice, and so has a person; you hear the bird and do as it does, and then you can learn to talk to it. But no, there is a limit; no doubt for the bird's sake, and for the sake of all the kinds of creatures which have voices, there was a limit to preserve their freedom. Man might oppress a wild creature, enslave it, kill it even – but never possess its soul. That meant he wasn't intended to!

Ryabinin tried hard to listen to the voices of the *taiga*, but the few natural sounds left in the section were overwhelmed by the remote noise of machinery. He even felt that the roar of the bulldozers was getting louder . . .

He cast a critical eye over the cabin, went inside and searched for something that still wanted fixing, but the rest needed major repairs: the stove, the ceiling, the floor. He went out and stood transfixed in bewilderment. The machines roared ever louder and – what was strange – nearer now, without a doubt. It was as if the bulldozers' roar were rolling towards him. Something frightful and incomprehensible infused his heart, making it work harder, as if defending itself against the onslaught of dread and dangerous forces.

The roaring now seemed to be coming from the very top of the rise. Ryabinin sensed the quaking of the earth and trees. The roaring felt like a motor whining wildly in his throat; was it the roaring of malevolent monsters, or the earth itself shouting in despair? He still couldn't work out what it all might mean. He was frozen like a statue in the cabin, and his beard quivered in response to his heart, which had lost its rhythm. And suddenly all the things which had happened that day came together, as if by magic, and the truth dawned on him. He groaned and clutched his head, then rushed off to find the hatchet and ran with all his might, ran to the place where at that moment the *Antichrist himself*, for centuries lurking in evil invisibility, had leapt out of the gloom and was hastening, full of hate, that he might destroy every living thing on the earth in the brief interval which God had allowed to him. Ryabinin ran up the rise, unaware that his heart could not keep up with his legs, not noticing the branches that lashed his face, the stones and mossy snags. He ran straight into obstacles, stumbled, fell, picked himself up and started running again. When he flew up the ridge, his heart flew still higher and dragged him up, up after it. So as not to take off completely, he seized a pine sapling in his hands, pressed himself to it and looked with horror at what had come to pass below, beneath his feet.

Small writhing demons had girded up other demons both mighty and frenzied, and were roaring towards the height, smashing to pieces everything in their path, leaving behind them two imperishable tracks of death!

Ryabinin saw:

ragged dirty people ripping to pieces a dying horse, convulsively chewing, jostling and beating each other with bloody pieces of meat;
falling wooden buttresses and clods of earth collapsing on people, crushing them, breaking arms and legs, flattening heads;
in a half-lit barracks, a tangled mass of dozens of bodies, shouts, blood, flashes of knives, shots from the window, dogs . . .

The images flashed before his eyes, dazzling him, scorching him, and tearing his heart out by the roots . . .

But what was happening was this:

The lads on the bulldozers were forcing their way towards the cabin. They wanted to appear ceremoniously before the mysterious old man, like *bogatyrs** of old on their mighty steeds. Crushing everything in their path, they had become quite beside themselves, like little children having a fierce game. But there was no malice in their hearts, and when the

* *bogatyr:* the knightly heroes of the Russian *bylina*, folk epic.

167

old man suddenly sprang up in front of them with maddened eyes, covered in scratches and blood, they froze to the spot.

Brandishing the axe, Ryabinin fell on the nearest bulldozer.

"What's with you, grandpa? What on earth are you doing?" yelled the driver, hurriedly jerking the control levers.

"Demons!" Ryabinin shouted so loud that the men on the second bulldozer could hear him.

"Psycho!" someone yelled and everyone flew off the bulldozers like the wind. The axe with the rubber handle recoiled off the metal, then found glass. Ivan Ryabinin tumbled down among the fragments. The hand holding the axe scrabbled at the earth and then all motion died away.

SIX

Selivanov stood at the edge of the road, waving his arms and cursing. An open truck slowed down but he waved it on; he wanted a saloon. A pirate taxi shot past without a glance at Selivanov. Then, despairing, he leapt out in front of a black Volga and it stopped. From it, without haste, emerged a strapping young lad. Stretching and flexing his biceps he strode towards the discomfited Selivanov and asked amiably, "What's your game, sweetheart?"

Every drop of blood left Selivanov's face but he stood his ground. "To Slyudyanka and back . . . to Luchikha and back . . . fifty roubles . . ."

"Get off!" the boy said in disbelief, "– in old money you mean?"

Selivanov drew a crisp new fifty out of his pocket. The lad scratched his head and looked at his watch.

"Well . . . want to chance it?"

Selivanov hopped into the back and huddled in the corner so that the driver could not see him in the mirror.

"Where are we going to in Slyudyanka?"

"The church."

"Get off! What . . . to die or repent?"

Selivanov lost his patience.

"Wash your filthy mouth out!"

The lad guffawed and put the radio on loud. Selivanov started to fidget, reached over and shouted venomously right into the driver's ear.

"If it's going to be like this all the way, take me straight to the morgue!"

The lad guffawed again, turned down the radio and bothered Selivanov no more.

The priest turned out to be young, tall and good looking, with a nice voice, and this threw Selivanov a bit.

"Scuse me, you see . . . like . . . a bloke died . . . a friend of mine . . ." his voice choked, "he was a believer in your god . . . He'd want everything done according to what's right."

"Where did the deceased live?" inquired the priest.

"Live?" Suddenly both eyes welled with tears. Selivanov brushed them away. "Far away . . . God forbid you should ever live in a place like that . . . but he's laid out at his home in Ryabinovka, so . . ." anticipating the priest, "I've got a car . . . I'll pay for it myself, whatever . . ."

They screeched off towards Ryabinovka. The driver sneaked a look at the priest in his rear view mirror and turned off the radio completely, only whistling from time to time.

"You, as I understand it, do not believe in God?" enquired the priest with delicacy.

"I can't believe in him since I can't find wisdom or goodness in Him!" replied a sullen Selivanov.

The priest looked at him quizzically but chose not to argue. Selivanov spoke again. "One man spends his whole life in sin and never even gets a splinter in his finger, another never kicked a dog once in his life but he gets all the troubles only a god like yours could think of."

The priest was silent.

"Then they say there's heaven in the next world . . . but who can prove it? I want to know, what did my pal Vanka Ryabinin suffer on this earth for? No answer to that, have you, God's servant?"

"There are no proofs," the priest answered quietly, "only faith can give you the answer."

"But if I need the answer in order to believe in the first

place? What's there for me to believe in if I don't have the answer to the main question?"

He broke down crying and banged a fist on his knee.

"I don't want to talk about anything. It's all rubbish!"

At the house, old women came out to meet the priest. A whole horde of them, as if every last corner of the earth had been emptied of old women. Leading them all, her eyes swollen from tears, was Svetlichnaya.

"To Luchikha!" Selivanov ordered the driver.

"To Luchikha it is!"

He pulled out in a cloud of dust.

"How people addle their brains with this shit about God! Can't think why the hell they keep on feeding those sodding priests!"

"Just as well you've got plenty of brawn, because you've got no brains," Selivanov responded.

"Hey grandad, I don't give a damn about your fifty! I should leave you wallowing in a ditch where you belong!"

"You just do that! Go on!" roared Selivanov, rising in his seat and throwing the banknote at the driver's feet. "Stop! I'm getting out! You may have shit for brains, but you might keep the stink to yourself! I'm telling you to stop!"

"What are you throwing money about for?" the driver raged. "You're got more money than sense . . . I'm going to throw you out and your money."

He hit the brakes so hard that Selivanov caught his chest on the back of the front seat. He jumped out and ran round to the driver's window and shouted, "Shit for brains!"

The driver caught up with him fifty yards from the car, grabbed his shoulder and stuck the banknote in the palm of his hand.

"Hey old man, it's your good luck that I don't hit old men like you! Take your money and get lost!"

"I'm not budging! I want to stay right here!!" roared Selivanov.

He wanted to fling the money in the driver's face, but the driver had his arm in a grip. Selivanov groaned and tore the banknote in half, then in quarters and then took advantage of the man's shock to hurl the tatters at him. The driver picked the tatters off the ground, stared at them and said indistinctly, "Why get upset? Fancy tearing up money – We'll go to your Luchikha . . . You said yourself, God wants . . ."

Selivanov calmed down.

"This boy'll be the death of me! I mean it, the death of me! I wish I was in my box!"

"Well, I know how you feel . . . your friend's died, and all . . ."

He went up to Selivanov and put a hand on his shoulder.

"Let's go or that boss of mine'll be wondering . . ."

The stuffing knocked out of him, Selivanov dragged himself to the car, crept on to the back seat and settled back with his eyes shut.

Behind the office of the farm processing plant, two-hundred-litre barrels were being loaded on to a tractor trailer. Obolensky was messing about nearby, sullen and grubby.

"You're coming with me!" shouted Selivanov, still a way off.

"No!" Obolensky shook his head, "off to the depot. I'm going down the Broad Dale sector, those barrels there . . ."

"F— your barrels! I'm telling you to come with me, the car's waiting!"

"Look at you!" Obolensky responded, delighted, noticing the Volga, "I can't, Selivanych! The boss already chewed my head off."

"You know I can fix it with the boss! Come here, before I drag you by the scruff of the neck!"

And that is exactly what he did.

"Oy, oy! Where are you going with him?" bellowed a man, emerging from behind the trailer – he was the director of the Broad Dale sector. "What, you gone daft Andrian Nikanorych?

I've got a ton of bilberries rotting in the *taiga*! It was God's own job getting that tractor off the boss!"

"You keep the tractor, it's him I want!" shouted Selivanov, dragging Obolensky, who'd dug his toes in, behind him. By the time Selivanov and Obolensky had reached the car, the two bosses – the factory manager as well as the director of the Broad Dale sector – had belted up from the porch of the office and fallen in at their side.

"Hey stop!" shouted the factory manager. "What's all this racket, Selivanov? Who do you think you are, giving orders? And you . . . back to your tractor!"

Selivanov grabbed Obolensky by the seat of his pants and dragged him back to the car.

"Stop yelling! I'm taking him to the *militsia*! He's up for murder! Understand?"

"What?" screeched Obolensky, eyes like saucers.

"Climb in the car!"

He bent Obolensky's head down and kneed him in the backside. The bosses swapped confused glances. Selivanov hopped into the car and slammed the door.

The car roared off.

A taxi was standing by the porch of the Ryabinin house, and Selivanov guessed that Natalya had arrived.

"Andrian Nikanorych! How can this possibly be? Why?"

"I'm to blame," he replied quietly, rubbing his eyes – not for the first time that day! "Shouldn't have let him go off into the *taiga* alone. He wasn't used to it, his heart couldn't take it. They say he just fell and that was it. An easy death, you can be grateful for that. He deserved an easy death though."

"And we'd never had our talk! Oh God! And we didn't give him a proper welcome!"

"Don't cry! Who knows, perhaps it was better for him like that. Don't cry!"

With a finger he wiped his eyes; she was shaking all over and choked with tears. Then, gently pushing Natalya aside,

Selivanov returned to the threshold, where Obolensky the tractor driver stood slouched. He led him into the room. On the table in the middle lay Ivan Ryabinin in his coffin. At his head stood the priest, wistful and pensive as he contemplated the mortal remains.

Elbowing the old women out of the way, Selivanov said loudly, "Come on, everyone, into the yard and get some fresh air, his kin want to pay their last respects."

The old women backed unwillingly towards the door, crossing themselves and whispering amongst themselves. Selivanov had broken with custom.

"See who's dead?" he turned sharply on the lad.

"Aha!" nodded Obolensky, "it's the old man who . . ."

"It's your father!"

"What d'you mean, father?" the tractor driver's voice was hoarse, almost a whisper.

"Yours, I'm telling you, your own flesh and blood, who was banished by the state to Satan's lair when you weren't yet born! Your mother had you and then wasted away there too for no good reason. That's why you grew up such a filthy little pillock, because you had no mother or father, only the state. As if you could grow up a man like that!"

The priest listened to Selivanov uneasily. Obolensky looked at the dead man with eyes wide open. The sound of footsteps and sobbing could be heard from behind. Natalya approached, her hands clutching at her throat. Her black shawl had unwound from her neck and fallen about her shoulders.

"And here . . ." said Selivanov taking her by the elbow and turning towards Obolensky, "this is your sister, which makes him your brother."

"What!" she moaned.

"He's called Ivan. His mother called him that after his father. Better she hadn't, though!"

Obolensky and Natalya looked at each other in horror.

"Selivanych, is that the truth?" whispered Obolensky.

"The truth, and worse than the truth . . ." he whispered

sadly and came round the coffin to stop at its head, next to the priest.

"Vanya, Vanya . . ." – his head was rocking back and forth. "Now I understand why life turned out like it did for you." He was silent. "It's you who have taken all my sins on yourself . . . paid for them . . . and died in my place before your time. My whole life I was wondering, trying to guess why I stuck to you, how I was tied to you. Yes, and I was too wicked to know that I'd been allowed to get near to a pure soul, for my own salvation!"

The priest quietly responded, "Each shall be held to answer for his own sins."

"He who has none shall take those of others on himself."

The priest crossed himself and fell silent.

"And suffering for your sins too . . ." Selivanov continued, nodding towards Natalya and Obolensky, ". . . he took that suffering on himself as well. And that wasn't all, I'll be bound: too much torment for one pure soul! But how can we repay him? Vanya! Vanya!"

Obolensky gave a cry and rushed out. Natalya ran after him.

"Don't despair," said the priest, "life is given by God and He knows for what purpose . . ."

"Yes, God knows . . . but he's not telling, is he! He's not even telling you! Well then, all the more reason why *I* won't be hearing anything from him!"

In the window a truck could be seen approaching, all decked out in black crape. Men jumped from the vehicle and started to lay a carpet of fir boughs.

"Well, look at that. They're paving the way Vanya . . . so you can make your last journey with the *taiga*'s fir needles beneath you . . . Would have been better if I'd died with you, wouldn't it . . ."

SEVEN

The sun was setting. Darkness already lay all around, but the village shone gold as the magic city ten leagues under the deep blue sea. The rowans shone brighter than anything, and through their leaves the lighted windows glowed like bonfires. The whole village was transformed, even the rusty handle of Ryabinin's well was gilded.

Selivanov sat on the step of the porch. He felt like a huge, unblinking eye which could see and observe everything going on, but which was quite detached from life. In an hour or two it would be dark, the people you could hear howling out songs in the house would be gone, and he would be alone with the night.

Sensing his glance, his dogs, which were chained up by the woodpile, twitched their tails a little, but he made no response. "Time I sold them!" he thought, and wasn't in the least startled that this dreadful idea had come into his head. Well, when you remembered what had happened when he'd thrown his handful of soil into the grave: there'd been a stone in it, and when it had hit the coffin, Selivanov had felt it like a blow on the heart. He was burying himself too. And when they'd taken the coffin out of the house he'd thought, "But it's way too long!" Why had he thought that? He was measuring it for himself, of course! And when they'd lowered the coffin into the grave, he couldn't bring himself to tell people to scatter the earth in. Not for ages . . . He'd wanted to lie down there too, hadn't he? Why else had he grumbled that the grave was too narrow, that the men had been lazy?

But there was something else on his mind which he couldn't twist into shape and which stopped him forming any conclusion on the problems of his life.

Obolensky staggered out of the *izba*. They'd given him a wash and a haircut and a change of clothes before the funeral, and he looked quite respectable until he opened his mouth. But you should have heard him swear, the bastard, when the corner of the coffin got caught in the door of the passage . . . Just as well for him he hadn't dropped it, or Selivanov would have knocked his block off for him.

Catching sight of Selivanov, Obolensky shambled up to him and stopped two paces away.

"Here, you, Selivanov. I'll never forgive you for this!"

"What's all this?"

"Why didn't you let on he was my father? What right had you to do that?"

"What right did *you* have to grow up into such a turd? Plenty of people get sent to orphanages and turn out all right, and just look what a pig you've turned out! I was ashamed to show you to your own father! Shouldn't be surprised if it was the sight of you made him go off and die in the *taiga*!"

"My whole life's a wreck!" Obolensky snivelled.

"Your choice. You can wreck your own life or you can put it together again, same as everyone else!" Selivanov growled and waved him away. "Go on, get your skinful, what's a holiday for! You can drink yourself blue in the face if you feel like it!"

"Suppose I don't feel like it today? Suppose I wish I was dead too?"

"Pull the other one!" Selivanov spat contemptuously. Then he suddenly came to life. "But maybe you really do wish you were dead. Eh?"

"Wha-a? I only . . ." said Obolensky without much conviction. Selivanov jumped up.

"Listen here, lad! Why should we stay here with nothing to do! Let's be off to Slyudyanka! There's a restaurant there, we'll make the band play so loud Ivan'll hear it from wherever it is he's gone to! His soul can fly anywhere in the world now, it can see everything, it can hear everything! There's nothing we can tell him by staying here!"

He grabbed hold of the boy's sleeve, and they set off at a brisk trot down from the house towards the forest road.

A huge cattle transporter swallowed them up in its cab and belted away from the sun, which was clinging to the tops of the pine trees as it sank.

As they rode along the old man and the snivelling youth sang dirty songs. The driver seemed inclined to take offence at first, but then he began to laugh and soon he was singing along. The bumpy ride wore Selivanov out, and every so often he would stop singing and ask dully, "Where are we going, then?" and the driver would bellow with laughter and shout, "To the *vytrezvitel*'*, so we can get you two dried out!" Half-way there they were overtaken by darkness. The driver switched on the headlights. When a car or motorbike coming from the other direction loomed up in the headlights, Selivanov would grab the driver by the sleeve and yell, "Squash him! Squash him, the rat, so he can't get in our light!" Obolensky was starting to nod off, so Selivanov elbowed him in the stomach. Obolensky gave a shriek, hit his forehead on the cab door, swore and fell asleep again. But Selivanov seemed to be scared of stopping his monkey tricks and fooling about, afraid of what would happen if he started being quiet and silent.

Every time something flew past them in the dark he yelled, and if the road was clear he spent the time cursing the driver and his lorry as loud as he could.

The lights of Slyudyanka appeared as they rounded a bend. The cold of the Lake Baikal evening flooded into the cabin and subdued Selivanov a little. Obolensky came to and muttered something inaudible.

---

* *vytrezvitel'*: police sobering station to which Soviet citizens are taken when drunk and disorderly.

"Where shall I put you down?" the driver asked.

"At the church," said Selivanov, to his own surprise.

Obolensky hiccoughed and jerked himself upright. The lorry accelerated across a pedestrian crossing, spraying front gardens and passers-by with muck, roared gingerly over a wobbly bridge and came to a halt outside the church. Selivanov gave the driver a hefty tip, showed Obolensky, still hiccoughing, out of the cabin and scrambled out himself.

"Well, so where is this restaurant?" Obolensky asked.

"Wait here!" Selivanov shouted and went off to the church gate. A light was burning above the porch, but there was a sturdy padlock on the door. Selivanov rattled it, scratching his head.

"Is it the father you're wanting, dearie?" asked an old woman's voice. "Look, that's his house there! But mass is over now," she continued eagerly. "Go on, go on! Knock at the door, there's no doggie there . . ."

Doggie indeed! Selivanov thought. – And here's me wanting to tear the throat out of something myself! He climbed up the two steps of the porch and banged on the door. Almost immediately he heard footsteps in the passage and the squeak of a bolt being drawn. Well, well, the pope can't be afraid of much, he hasn't asked who I am. Suppose I had a club on me?

"What do you want?" asked the priest, not recognising Selivanov in the feeble light of the bulb.

"But it's me!"

"Ah! I didn't recognise you. Come in!"

"No, no!" said Selivanov hastily and shrank with embarrassment. "Well, you see, like, it's in memory of my friend, see . . ." And he abruptly thrust his hand into his pocket, brought out a pile of crumpled notes and handed them to the priest.

"What's this!" The priest stepped back. "You've given me more than you should in any case!"

"It's not that I want! It's for him, in memory of him! Eternal memory! What I mean to say is, how much would it cost . . . so that every day . . ."

The priest shook his head.

"I can't possibly take it! You must see the treasurer. He'll make a receipt out for you."

"I don't want him to have it! I want you to! If you don't take it I'll tear it up and throw it all round the church!"

The priest was shaken.

"But I've got no right."

"Well, then I have. It's up to you, if you don't want it I'll chuck it away! Your god'll understand why my conscience . . ."

Selivanov walked down the porch steps.

"Hang on!" shouted the priest in despair.

"Are you going to take it or not?"

"How much are you giving me?"

"I'm not a cat, am I, so how can I see in the dark? Take it or leave it!"

"All right, I'll count it and enter it in the accounts and let you know . . ."

"You're not a priest," Selivanov said, "you're a bloody accountant from a meat factory! I'm telling you that I'm dying, my soul's halfway out of my body, and you give me 'enter in the parish accounts'."

Selivanov cursed, shoved the money at the priest and, throwing up his hands, strode off to the gate. But before he got there, he stopped and ran back again.

"Listen, there's something you can do for me, whatever the right thing is, like. I may have gone to the bad, but just say a quick prayer for me, will you . . . just in case."

The priest stuffed the money into his pocket, stepped right up to Selivanov and made the sign of the cross over him.

"Blessing me, are you? What's the good of that? When I was a little lad, my mother used to drag me along to go through all that, I mean so I should live my life in the right way, see. But what good is it now, when I've had my life?"

The priest interrupted him.

"If you're ever in Slyudyanka, I do hope you'll drop in. Any time. Please do!"

"It's a bit late for that now! Goodbye to you!"

"Are we going to the restaurant, then?" Obolensky asked in a whining voice.

"Yes, it really is high time we got there!" Selivanov said. But a little further on he suddenly stopped in front of a certain building. Next to the door glittered a plaque. The lighted windows had curtains at them, and shadows flittered across the curtains.

"Well now!" Selivanov ground out, surprised and annoyed. "So they work a late shift, do they! And fancy where they've set themselves up, too, right by God's back door! Wait here!" he ordered Obolensky.

The first door opened on a short passageway. At the end was a second door; it was locked, and on it was the eye-catching pink button of a bell. Selivanov pressed it. A tall young man in a grey suit opened it. He was wearing a tie and looked spick and span, not a hair out of place.

"What do *you* want, grandad?" he asked, surprised.

Selivanov hunched his back, leaned over sideways and wrinkled his face.

"Well, see, I want the what's its name, I mean the ogeepeeyoo. Here, is it?"

"What?" said the young man, astonished.

"I'm telling you, the ogeepeeyoo . . ."

"Where have *you* been all this time? There's been no ogeepeeyoo for forty years and more!"

"Well I never!" said Selivanov, clapping his hands and even bending his knees in his amazement. "So there isn't one! But whoever heard of that, don't tell me the powers that be can get by without their ogeepeeyoo? Not having an old man on, are you?"

The young man put his hands in his pockets. His expression becoming slightly colder, he explained in a condescending tone:

"Yes, it was called the ogeepeeyoo in the old days, but now it's called the kaygeebee, KGB, the Committee for State Security."

"Kay-ay, gee-ee, bee-ee." Selivanov drawled thoughtfully. "My, the names they think up for themselves! Fair takes your breath away!"

"What *do* you want, grandad?"

By now the young man's tone was extremely cold.

"Phooey, what do you think, I want the boss! I've got something really important to talk over with him. Which door do you keep him behind, then?"

The young man involuntarily glanced at a door on the left, and Selivanov made straight for it. A well-scrubbed white palm stopped him.

"The boss is busy. Tell me. I'll pass it on."

"We-ell, maybe I could do that," moaned Selivanov, crestfallen. "But excuse me for asking, what rank do you hold?"

"Full lieutenant."

Selivanov drew himself up and swept his eyes contemptuously over the young man.

"Lieutenant, eh!" he said indignantly. "And here I am wasting my time with you! Pooh!"

Skirting round the young man, he shouldered the door open and closed it behind him.

In the room a man of about forty was sitting in an armchair at the head of a long table and writing something. He too was in a suit and tie. Without giving him a chance to open his mouth, Selivanov burst out: "'Scuse me, I'm sure, but I was just going past, I saw your light on, I realised you were working night shift, here's my chance, I thought, ar, and I've a little question I'd be glad if you'd answer, because it's the most important thing in the world for me. So will you hear an old man out!"

"What's the matter?" asked the boss sternly.

"What I mean to say is, I mean what I want to know . . . the power of the Soviets, what we have now, how long will our dear Soviet power go on overpowering us?"

"What's your name?"

"My name, you say?" said Selivanov, smiling broadly. "You can't get by without a name for long, I know that! Well, my name's Selivanov, Andrian Nikanorych Selivanov! And what's yours, if you don't mind telling me?"

"Drunk, are you?" the boss snapped.

"I've had one or two!" Selivanov agreed with alacrity.

"Have you got your papers on you?"

Selivanov seemed to have been waiting for this. He sprang forward at once to proffer the boss his internal passport. The boss glanced at the first page and then at the signature and returned it.

"Go and sleep it off for now. We can have our little chat about the Soviet state in the morning."

Selivanov seemed not to notice the threatening tone in the boss's voice. "Tomorrow? Yes, that'll be fine! Do you really mean it? It'll make all the difference between life and death for me."

"Get out!" roared the boss and banged his fist on the table.

Bowing and scraping, Selivanov backed to the door. As he left the building he heard the boss shout "Kaurov!" And out of the corner of his eye he saw the lieutenant rushing into the office.

Obolensky's face swam towards him out of the darkness.

"Yeah?"

"Let's go! Time's getting on, and we've still got to get pissed tonight!"

Obolensky burst out laughing.

"And what were you doing in there, Selivanov, eh?"

"I asked them when their Soviet power would collapse!"

Obolensky shut up as though he'd swallowed his tongue, and said nothing for a long time.

A dozen or so youngsters – boys and girls – were hanging round the entrance to the restaurant. On the glass panel of the door hung a sign saying "Full". Selivanov wormed his way through to the door and banged on it. Behind the glass appeared the pompous visage of a doorman in livery which looked like a dog's harness. Selivanov pressed his palm to the glass. The doorman stretched out his face, and his hands twitched rapidly along the door handle. Then the magic palm skipped lightly from the glass and smacked the doorman's hand. He froze only for a moment, but just long enough to allow Selivanov and Obolensky to force their way in through the half-open door.

They went up to the room on the first floor, where a band was playing its guts out whilst a few couples gyrated in the cramped space between the rows of tables. The waitresses were rushing hither and thither, looking like white daisies in their smoky and garish setting. Selivanov left Obolensky by the doorway and darted off somewhere on the far side of the tables. He must have done a few shady deals there, for as a result a free table for two materialised.

Selivanov waved, and Obolensky rushed smartly up to the table, just as the band began pounding out its tunes again. The drummer clashed his cymbals so loudly it sounded as if he'd crashed the floor and ceiling together, turning his listeners to speechless jelly in the middle. Obolensky stared around him like a zombie. Selivanov sat there morosely beating a fork on his plate and moving his lips (he was soundlessly cursing everything he could see). At the next table there were three lads hardly out of short trousers and a young female of about the same age. They jerked all their limbs in time to the drummer's beat, staring at each other with foggy eyes and elbowing each other in the ribs; from time to time they seized each other's hands. Obolensky looked at them with envy,

Selivanov with disgust. But the lads and the girl had no eyes for them.

The carafes of vodka and cognac which they'd ordered were brought to the table, together with fancy meatballs, salads and even napkins; these last Selivanov fastidiously pushed away to the far end of the table.

When their glasses had been filled, Selivanov was about to make a toast. Instead, no sooner had he opened his mouth than he swore and went up to the band.

The band almost froze on the note and launched into a mournful number about the vagrant who escaped from prison on Sakhalin island. Only monstrous generosity on Selivanov's part could have inclined them to such heroism.

"Let's drink to my friend, to your father! May he have a new life beyond this one, may the earth not swallow him up, may he rise above it and fly off the f— knows where!"

Obolensky greedily swallowed the meatballs. Selivanov watched him munching and swilling down drink and said gloomily:

"You know, you're called Ivan too, but I can't bring myself to call you that! Vanka's the most I can manage. You were more of an Ivan in your mother's womb than you are now."

Obolensky smiled through a mouthful of food, grabbed the carafe and poured himself another shot. He was softening visibly round the edges, losing control of himself. Suddenly he burst into tears.

"Doesn't make no difference, I'll still never forgive you. Why didn't you tell me about my father?"

"Belt up!" Selivanov snarled.

"I'll tell you what I'll do to you!" babbled Obolensky drunkenly. "I'll run you over in my tractor an' I'll push the button and turn it round and round so you get mashed into the ground with the caterpillar! That's what I'll do to you!"

"Silly git," said Selivanov listlessly.

185

"I'll run you over in my tractor."

Selivanov refilled Obolensky's glass.

"I want to sing!" he announced.

"Sing then, you silly cow."

Obolensky leapt up, attracting the attention of all their neighbours, and, opening his eyes like saucers, began bawling hideously:

OOOH my little witch!
Just you watch her twitch!
She goes walking tittity-tup,
Wish she'd let me feel her up!

He couldn't remember any more of the words, so he shouted "E-e-eh!" and jumped up and down on the spot, waving his legs in the air (this meant he was dancing). The lads from the next table surrounded him, clapping their hands and winking at one another; they were helpless with laughter.

"Selivanov, mate!" wailed Obolensky. "I want to treat them!" Without saying anything, Selivanov got 25 roubles out of his jacket pocket and flung them on the table.

'I'll treat everyone! I've a right to!'

The boys hugged Obolensky and slapped him on the back. Dragging him off to their table, they put him on the girl's knee. She tickled him and let him paw her.

Selivanov sat in sullen solitude, drinking steadily but not managing to get drunk.

Another 25 roubles made its way from his pocket to the next table; the squeals and shrieks coming from there almost drowned the band. The manager appeared and said something to the lads, pointing to the door.

Selivanov got up, threw down another 25 roubles on the table, went up to the group and dragged Obolensky off the girl. The boys tried to object, but he silenced them with a curt: "Shoo, you puppies!" They exchanged venomous glances, but said nothing.

Half-carrying Obolensky, he took him out of the restaurant. It was dark and cold. Obolensky broke away, shouting, "Don't want to!" but Selivanov landed him a punch and he began to snivel.

"We'll go to the station, we can kip down there until the bus comes . . . Well, my wake for my friend turned out no good. Get on then, you stupid git! I've had more than I can take of you already!"

There was a light-bulb hanging above the restaurant entrance and one or two on telegraph posts further on. Beyond that, darkness. They groped their way forward with weaving gait. What was the hurry, anyway? At the end of an alley near the station was another light-bulb on a crooked post. By some miracle it had stayed alight. It was here they found themselves eyeball to eyeball with the boys from the restaurant. Their floosie wasn't with them now.

"Right, grandad, turn out your pockets!" hissed one of them, giving Selivanov a shove.

"Wha-a-a-?" He was too winded to say more. Obolensky came to that instant and stepped back into the darkness.

"Turn out your pockets!" repeated another boy, adopting a bass voice.

"You mangy young puppies!" Selivanov was panting with rage. "You, giving me this? Do you know who I am? No, bet your life you don't, you woodlice, you've never seen anything like me, not even in the pictures. Vanka!"

But Obolensky had vanished into thin air. The boys stood there with crooked grins on their faces, shifting their hands in their pockets.

"Turn out your pockets, you old sod, or we'll beat your piles to pulp!"

Selivanov was shaking.

"Are you trying to scare me, you little weasel? The men from the Cheka managed that, they scared me into the ground! The powers that be scared me all right, till they got fed up bothering with me! But you . . . Be off with you, shoo, you half-baked young twerps!"

Selivanov saw stars. He jerked backwards, but stayed on his feet. The second blow hit his head, and someone grabbed him from behind, whilst someone else rifled his pockets.

"Anything there?"

"Yeah."

"Bastards!" yelled Selivanov. "I'll smack you so hard you can't sit down!"

"Sanka, just shut the old swine up before he squeals the place down, will you?" Selivanov felt a savage blow in the side. His knees gave way and when they let him go, down he went.

The alley was deserted. It hurt too much to get up. He felt his side and his fingers came away wet. Suddenly he realised they'd stabbed him. Yes, of course! It was running down his thigh. And the smell, he knew that smell. "What's this?" Selivanov wondered. "Have they done me in, those puppies?" The outrage of it dulled his pain. And suddenly he said with relief: "Well, thank God for that then! Christ, what reason have I got to go on living! Now I'll just peg out here under this fence. It was meant!"

He wanted to lie on his back, like a human being, whilst he was still in his right mind, so he could breathe freely. He lay in the middle of the alley, squeezing his wound, and gazed at the sky. And he imagined how someone would come down the alley in the morning, see his corpse and get the fright of their lives . . .

But will there be anyone to bury me? The thought struck him all of a sudden. – No one'll tell them in Irkutsk, after all . . . So this is what it's come to! He sobbed quietly. God, it's too much!

Death still wasn't here. Not here, the bitch! She wanted to torment him, to let him be killed by his sense of affront, not his wound; she wanted to make him curse his life, to make him beg to hurry up, the sleazy slut, so that when she came at last he would call it a blessing.

But you shouldn't give these dark thoughts anything to feed on, better to cheat them by turning towards the light . . .

"Eh, Ivan, lad!" he whispered. "If you're out there some-where, I bet you'll be pleased; won't be long now till we see each other again . . . Not likely, though: after all, I'll be going to the other place, won't I? Will you say a prayer for me, now? You know I never did you nothing but good! Never mind that buckshot, eh – didn't even leave a scar. A wound in the leg's one thing, a wound in the side's another, after all. And even in the side you can stand it, look at me now."

Suddenly he was sure he could hear Ivan laughing. But you couldn't see him anywhere . . .

Wasn't it unfair, Ivan laughing at him, when death was staring him in the face?

His back was getting stiff. The ground was covered in pebbles, and you could feel the cold coming off it. Selivanov fidgeted. And suddenly he realised, "P'raps I'm not hurt so bad after all."

Hardly had he digested this thought than he was on his feet. There was a stabbing, pinching, crushing pain in his side. Down his leg was a stream of blood right to the heel. But he wasn't dead yet, was he?

"There's a dog's life for you," he said loudly. "Not even allowed to die when you want to . . ."

He gave a preoccupied nod and, squeezing the wound with his hand, hobbled swiftly off towards the station.